THE NINTH  ES

Interview with the Last

AMERICAN PRESIDENT

HALIM RASHAD

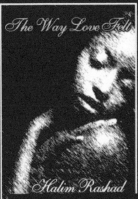

The Way Love Felt

Halim Rashad

HALIM RASHAD
NAMI SIGNATURE SERIES

A QUIET EXISTENCE
IN A
SILENT HELL
THE PRIVATE LETTERS OF A
TORTURED MAN

NAMI PUBLISHING PRESENTS

THE NINTH NAMI GROUND SERIES
PUBLISHING

Interview with the Last
AMERICAN PRESIDENT

HALIM RASHAD

BLURRED REPHLEKSHUNZ
The Foul Doctrine Vol. I

MA
MATURE READERS ONLY

HALIM RASHAD

BLURRED REPHLEKSUNZ
VOLUME II
THE ART OF WORD
2003-2007

THE

nami publishing presents

THE WHITE BOOK
A COLLECTION OF SHORT STORIES

HALIM RASHAD
HR
BOROUGHS

HALIM
RASHAD

FROM THE STREETOLOGY SERIES
MAHOGANY
CHASE

NAMI

THE NINTH GROUND
OPERATION SERPENT EAGLE

THE CONCLUSION TO "INTERVIEW WITH THE LAST AMERICAN PRESIDENT"

HALIM RASHAD

From "The White Book (The Five Boroughs)"
A collection of short stories.

****

OF "THE NINTH GROUND" SERIES

INTERVIEW WITH THE LAST
AMERICAN PRESIDENT

AUTHORED BY **HALIM RASHAD**

THIS STORY IS INTENDED FOR A MATURE AUDIENCE ONLY.

NAMI PUBLISHING
BROOKLYN • MANHATTAN • STATEN ISLAND • QUEENS • THE BRONX

THIS IS BOOK IS DEDICATED TO:
My wife & children, to the English Department at Buffalo State College
and then to the future.

Not just my future, but also that of my family, my community,
my society, our societies, and the global community.
When we imagine what this world can be, why can we not imagine achieving that dream?
Jehovah put us here for a reason, achieve the dream to make this world one
the Devil cannot run upon freely.

TABLE OF CONTENTS

Book, cover & design by the Author.
Authentic authorized copies of this book is available for sale:
Charles G. Smith III c/o Nami Publishing,
Buffalo, NY
P. (716) 545-3399   Internet: www.sheddingink.com

NAME: DAVID JACKSON GLASS   **ALIAS:** JACKSON GLASS

GENDER: MALE

DOB: JANUARY 21ST, 2028   **AGE:** 28

HEIGHT: 5'10"   **WEIGHT:** 180 LBS.   **EYES:** GREY   **COMPLEXION:** LIGHT

ETHNICITY: MIXED: AFRICAN-AMERICAN AND CAUCASIAN

POB: SYRACUSE, NEW YORK

CURRENT RESIDENCE: PITTSBURGH, PA

OCCUPATION: FREELANCE INVESTIGATIVE REPORTER

SPECIAL SKILLS/TRAINING: PILOT; MILITARY TRAINING IN WEAPONS, COMBAT, & ARCHERY

MISSION: BEGAN AS AN INTERVIEW WITH FORMER PRESIDENT RICHARD BRIDGES AND BECAME A RECONNAISSANCE MISSION TO COLLECT INFORMATION THAT WOULD EXPOSE THE RULING BODIES OF THE AMERICAN GOVERNMENT TO THE PUBLIC.

LINEAGE: US AIR FORCE CAPT. DAVID MALIK GLASS, (BLACK) & BRIDGET GLASS (CAUCASIAN) HIGH SCHOOL ENGLISH TEACHER.

NAME: RICHARD TOBIAS BRIDGES   **ALIAS:** SERPENT EAGLE

GENDER: MALE

DOB: NOVEMBER 11TH, 1996 **AGE:** 60

HEIGHT: 6'   **WEIGHT:** 207 LBS.   **EYES:** BROWN   **COMPLEXION:** BROWN

ETHNICITY: AFRICAN-AMERICAN

POB: HOUSTON, TEXAS

CURRENT RESIDENCE: RICHARD M. NIXON FEDERAL PENITENTIARY, OUTSIDE OF PRESQUE ISLE, MAINE

OCCUPATION: FORMER U.S. PRESIDENT, FORMER CAPTAIN IN THE US AIR FORCE & ASSISTANT DISTRICT ATTORNEY

SPECIAL SKILLS/TRAINING: MILITARY BACKGROUND, POLITICS & LAW

MISSION: EXPOSE HAMES AS A CRIMINAL; CLEAR HIS NAME AND RESTORE AMERICA TO ITS FORMER STATE.

LINEAGE: FATHER WAS A CONSTRUCTION WORKER AND MOTHER WAS A PARALEGAL.

NAME: EDWARD KING HAMES   ALIAS: NONE

GENDER: MALE

DOB: MARCH 10TH,1998   AGE: 58

HEIGHT: 6' 2" WEIGHT: 198 LBS.   EYES: BLUE

ETHNICITY: CAUCASIAN

POB: SARASOTA, FLORIDA

CURRENT RESIDENCE: WASHINGTON D.C.

OCCUPATION: U.S. SENATOR (CONGRESSIONAL PRESIDENT THEREFORE THE REAL POWER IN THE GOVERNMENT), & FORMER AIR FORCE FIGHTER PILOT

SPECIAL SKILLS/TRAINING: MILITARY

MISSION: TO SEIZE COMPLETE CONTROL OF U.S. GOVERNMENT IN ORDER TO AUTHORIZE THE SURRENDER OF THE COUNTRY TO THE COMMUNIST GOVERNMENT OF RUSSIA. HE FEELS THAT A RUSSIAN INVASION IS INEVITABLE AND HAS SECRETLY CONVINCED THE CONGRESS THAT THE BEST COURSE OF ACTION IS AN UNCONDITIONAL SURRENDER. HE HAS BARGAINED TO ALLOW HIMSELF AND CERTAIN CONRGESSIONAL MEMBERS TO REMAIN IN POWER UNDER THE RED PARTY. ALL THAT REMAINS AN OBSTACLE IS IF THIS INFORMATION WAS TO BE MADE PUBLIC PRIOR TO ALL FINAL ARRANGEMENTS, HE FEARS CIVIL WAR WILL BREAK OUT AND THE GOVERNMENT (HIMSELF) WILL BE OVER THROWN AND PUNISHED.

NAME: UNKNOWN   ALIAS: TRINI

GENDER: MALE

DOB: UNKNOWN   AGE: UNKNOWN

HEIGHT: 6' 6" WEIGHT: 219 LBS.   EYES: BLUE   COMPLEXION: TAN BROWN

ETHNICITY: UNKNOWN

POB: FORTALEZA, BRAZIL

CURRENT RESIDENCE: WASHINGTON D.C.

OCCUPATION: HEAD OF HAMES' HIRED ASSASSINS KNOWN AS "THE PLUMBERS". A GROUP OF SOUTH AMERICAN MEN, NOTORIOUS FOR COMMITING MURDERS, AND VARIOUS OTHER CRIMES.

SPECIAL SKILLS/TRAINING: DETAILS ARE UNKNOWN: CIA TRAINED IN COMBAT, AND ESPIONAGE.

MISSION: TO CARRY OUT ANY AND ALL ORDERS DELEIVERED BY HAMES. USUALLY INVOLVES EXECUTING POLITICIANS OR UNOFFICIAL ENEMIES OF THE STATE.

NAME: CHARLES MAXIMILIAN ASHMAN   **ALIAS:** CHESTER

GENDER: MALE

DOB: OCTOBER 19TH, 2027   **AGE:** 29

HEIGHT: 5' 8"   **WEIGHT:** 235 LBS.   **EYES:** BROWN

ETHNICITY: CAUCASIAN

POB: MANCHESTER, ENGLAND

CURRENT RESIDENCE: BUFFALO, NY

OCCUPATION: COMPUTER INFORMATION SYSTEMS SPECIALIST

SPECIAL SKILLS/TRAINING: SOFTWARE DESIGN & COUNTERFEIT

MISSION: TO HELP JACKSON ESCAPE AUTHORITIES.

NAME: ELIJAH KNIGHT   **ALIAS:** KNIGHT

GENDER: MALE

DOB: UNKNOWN   **AGE:** UNKNOWN

HEIGHT: 6' 2"   **WEIGHT:** 178 LBS.   **EYES:** BROWN

ETHNICITY: CAUCASIAN

POB: UNKNOWN

CURRENT RESIDENCE: UNKNOWN

OCCUPATION: CIA AGENT / DOUBLE AGENT ALSO WORKING FOR BRIDGES

SPECIAL SKILLS/TRAINING: CIA TRAINING IN ALL AREAS OF ESPIONAGE, COMBAT, WEAPONS, LIE DETECTION, AND MUCH, MUCH MORE

MISSION: TO AID BRIDGES IN HIS QUEST TO SAVE AMERICA FROM, WELL, ITSELF. HE IS ASSIGNED TO ACT AS LIASON BETWEEN BRIDGES AND GLASS AND BECOMES GLASS' BODYGUARD.

NAME: UNKNOWN   **ALIAS:** Q

GENDER: FEMALE

DOB: UNKNOWN   **AGE:** UNKNOWN

HEIGHT: 5' 9" **WEIGHT:** 143 LBS. **EYES:** BROWN   **COMPLEXION:** LIGHT

ETHNICITY: AFRICAN-AMERICAN/JAPANESE

POB: HAMPTON, VA

CURRENT RESIDENCE: N/A

OCCUPATION: CIA AGENT ACTING AS A DOUBLE AGENT AIDING BRIDGES

SPECIAL SKILLS/TRAINING: ALMOST SAME AS KNIGHT; NOT AS EXTENSIVE.

MISSION: Q WORKS FOR HAMES AND HAS BEEN INSTRUCTED TO FIND OUT WHAT GLASS KNOWS, HIS MISSION AND STOP HIM IF HE POSES A THREAT.

MINOR CHARACTERS

Warden Atkins

Rebecca Watkins-Glass, Jackson's ex-wife

Carlton Fanning, undercover henchman of Atkins'

Ronald Harris, CIA Director

Det. Stephen Brown, Buffalo Police Department

INTRODUCTION

At the dawn of the 21st Century, the 43rd President of the United States, George W. Bush and his administration, unknowingly set in motion the players that would dramatically change the world forever.

Though Bush had left office two terms ago, the Presidents to follow would inherit his war. In 2014, the "unwinnable" and disastrous "War on Terror" was declared over. The 44th President pulled American troops out of Iraq, Afghanistan, Iran, and Syria in his second term. The war Bush planned against North Korea never materialized, instead it was "postponed" to a much later date. The next President elected to office decided that it was time for America to focus on homeland security and place more attention on an economy that was still recovering from the Bush Administration.

By 2016, the leaders of all Arab-speaking Middle Eastern countries secretly forged an alliance they called *The Union of Taqwa* (Taqwa meaning "to guard against danger") to present a united front against future attacks and invasions. Simultaneously, the economy of the Russian Federation had finally collapsed. After twenty years of attempting to establish a Capitalistic/Democratic society in this country whose people were still adapting to life without Communism, the struggle overcame the government. Over the years, the party remained strong throughout Russia, despite the efforts of several Presidents. In 2017, one year into their own Great Depression, the Communist Party staged a bloody coup, killing the President, the Vice President, and any Federation loyalists staffed inside the Kremlin. The body of the Russian leader was strung up in the country's capital, at the foot of the Bolshoi Theater steps in Sverdlova Square, for all to see for several days and was eventually burned.

At the U.N., tensions were higher than usual because of this uprising. Many knew the Red Party sought revenge for its defeat in the late 20th Century. The new Russian leaders would not sit with the U.N. for more than two years. During that time, American spy planes discovered what the Communist leaders were up to in their isolation. It was eventually revealed that the Russians were rebuilding their nuclear arms, strengthening their military, and quietly seizing control of most of Eastern Europe bringing up the "Iron Curtain" yet again.

Between 2021 and 2028, Russia was engaged in battle after bloody battle, victorious in each, taking control of the defeated governments and brought them under the Red flag of Communism. China aligned itself with Russia and helped to conquer the entire continent of Asia and much of Indonesia. As the Communist Alliance swallowed India and Thailand, North Korea was convinced that it would be in their best interest to join Russia and China. This alliance allowed South Korea to fall under the North's rule in time. Next, Communism declared a lengthy and disastrous war on *The Union of Taqwa* that did not end until the Union was defeated in 2028. By this time, the Communist Alliance successfully conquered continental Asia and neighboring islands, except Japan. While this was taking place, the United States Congress refused to intervene, against the President's urging. In 2030, Russia unleashed its fury upon Germany, simultaneously, the combined military forces of China and Korea attacked Japan and US Navy battleships sent to protect the country. The US Congress had no choice but to officially declare war on the aggressors, giving the President the necessary authority to take on Communism. They knew it was only a matter of time before Russia would seek to over take all of Europe and then North America.

Within five years, America's resources were nearly depleted, military spent and the draft was in effect once more. Patriotism was high but not many youths wanted to leave high school to fight a two front war. America, however, did not stand alone against its enemies; early in the war England, France, Switzerland, Canada, Spain, Italy, Portugal, Ireland, Turkey, Egypt, Jordan and most of the countries of Africa allied themselves with the US in order to thwart the Communist Alliance's plans for global domination. Though *The Union of Taqwa* had fallen, there were many that wished their new occupiers gone. Insurgency ran rampant throughout the Arab world, while it would appear that most of Asia had simply given up, India engaged in guerilla warfare attacking Russian posts and small groups of soldiers under the cloak of the night. Crude oil producing countries unanimously decided to destroy all their oil wells in order to prevent the Communists from controlling the world's oil resources and eliminate any future economic gain to the occupying governments.

World War III was officially over and a cease-fire was announced in 2042. The political borders of many nations changed and some countries simply did not exist anymore. The United States of America lost a much as it gained: Alaska, Hawaii, Guam, most of its territories was captured and nearly half of the American population was killed. Cuba attacked the islands of the Caribbean and gained sympathizers throughout Central America and South America as well. In order to prevent losing the territory of Puerto Rico to Communism, the island nation was officially made a state. The army of Mexico, being a sympathizer to the Communist Movement, attacked the US border, but was eventually forced into submission. Mexico was later annexed by the US and made a territory. Captured South and Central American leaders and generals were put to death without a tribunal or any form of trial. The Communist Alliance gained France, Germany, Italy, Turkey, the Netherlands, Iceland, and Greenland was officially declared as Communist nations. Most of Western Europe remained unscathed. Russia and its allies maintained their hold on all they had conquered, suffering only loss of lives. Canada's border was reduced by thirty-five percent, losing half of its northern region and a quarter of the northwestern region ending at Kitimat in British Columbia; coming very close to the US border. During the war, the U.N. was dissolved, as it could no longer maintain order and many of the US's allies sided with the Communist Alliance for fear of being assassinated.

The United States of America suffered, as New York City, Los Angeles, Hollywood, Miami Seattle, and San Antonio were either ravaged, war torn or leveled. In spite of the destruction, the American people came together to rebuild their nation and assess what is to become of its new additions. The American military put down the Cuban government, led by Fidel Castro's grandson. Many countries in South America turned Communist either through elections or by force.

At 7:18 pm August 28th 2042, the President ordered thirty 3rd generation Stealth Bombers F-119C, and twenty fighter jets to fly into Chinese airspace and launch their nuclear missiles onto China's capital, Beijing. A Naval fleet of some twenty-eight ships was located between Japan's coast and Korea, in the Sea of Japan. The jets took off and made a daring attempt to make it to their destination. Forty minutes into the battle that ensued, only three Stealth Bombers made it to Beijing and then after a series of unpreventable Kamikaze attacks by the Chinese fighters, only one American Bomber was left. Beijing and surrounding towns and villages as far as far north as Shenyang and as south as Zhengzhou were completely vaporized. The blast killed many people, including the Prime Minister of the Chinese government; Russia's greatest ally. President Richard W. Bridges, (a Republican from Texas and former Captain in the U.S. Air Force) became the President that ended the war, by launching nuclear bombs on Beijing.

He was the only of the five Presidents that inherited this war, to put a stop to the Communist Alliance. Bridges' first term was not swamped with corruption and scandals, as those that preceded him. Bridges maintained order throughout America saying that the people of America "had to accept that the Communist Alliance would keep what they've gained. But the United States will march on and rebuild our lives and our country after this terrible war." Over 100 million people including soldiers and civilians were killed in this twenty-one year war. With America's wealth greatly exhausted, the country suffered a recession delving ever closer to a depression.

Bridges went on to win a second term by a landslide as "America's Peacekeeper". However, before the President had time to worry about an economic break down, a reporter from the Washington Post uncovered the sordid details of what was believed to have been Bridges' "true war record". It was discovered that while serving in the air force during the fall of 2032, Bridges, then a Captain flying bomber jets known as "Eagle's Talon K-35", patrolling the borders of Israel, fired four missiles into a camp set up in the desert just near the Israeli-Jordanian border, along the Jordan River and the Dead Sea. He claimed this base was the enemy's camp. An investigation revealed that the camp was actually a base for civilian insurgents fighting against the Communist Alliance. Bridges attested that the camp had the red flag of Communism waiving and determined it was a military post. The cover up of the misdeed seemed to have been more important to the people than the actual act. This was the first of many scandals to rip through his administration, during his second term.

The next and most condemning of the accusations was that members of his administration and the Republican Party, under Bridges' instruction, worked together to place followers and sympathizers on the Electoral College. People were placed among the Electors in states that did not have laws dictating that the College had to vote in accordance to their state's popular vote, a law that still existed in only eleven of the fifty-four states by this time. A federal investigation resulted; revealing that this accusation was not only real, but also the crime was committed during both elections. Thus, the impeachment process had begun. Bridges was charged with:

1. Treason,

2. Defrauding the American Government,

3. Tampering with a Federal election,

4. Conduct unbecoming (as he was a sitting President),

5. Bribery,

6. Obstruction of Justice,

7. Perjury (which was added later by the Senate).

Additional charges were filed by each state in which the offense was committed. Upon the House of Representatives' approval of the articles of impeachment, the Senate began the impeachment process on January 18th 2045. Certain members of Bridges' cabinet were charged, tried, and convicted of charges stemming from defrauding the government and Treason.

On May 20th 2046, President Richard Wilson Bridges became the third US President to have been impeached and the first to have been convicted of a crime; he was subsequently removed from office and sentenced to never hold a political office. The Senate did not stop there however; Bridges was sentenced to life in federal prison for the charge of treason, as committed in each individual state throughout the country.

Because of Bridges' conviction, the Congress successfully seized the powers of the Executive branch, citing the corruption the position has suffered over nearly three hundred years. The Congress did not simply amend the US Constitution; instead, they re-wrote the document to authorize the Congress to hold the powers of creating, enacting laws, and enforcing policy. The office of the President became a less authoritative position that held very limited powers, which no longer included the power to veto.

Furthermore, the responsibilities of a President were divided into a Pluralist system similar to Canada, between a President that would conduct domestic affairs and one that would conduct foreign affairs. The Presidents were to carry out foreign affairs and enforce laws passed by Congress and upheld by the Supreme Court. Presidential elections were cancelled from then on; the Presidents would permanently be selected, confirmed, and appointed by the Congress. The overhaul of the US Government did not stop at there. In the new Constitution, Congress eliminated natural American citizen's dual citizenship between federal and state governments. States lost most of its powers as the federal government increased many of its powers becoming a Federalist nation.

In order to make this happen though, the government compromised with the American populace, doing away with the Capitalistic economic system and establishing a more Socialist system in nature; increasing federal aid for education, and other important areas to the people. For the first time the people forced the government to enact laws that would allow the members of Congress to be held accountable for their actions and be punished not through elections, but immediate removal from office and replaced, as determined by a vote by the people. The new Constitution was subsequently ratified (by the people, not the states), on December 11th, 2055.

Today, Bridges, the convict, is still serving his sentence as an example for future politicians, isolated from the prison population. This is where our story begins.

CHAPTER ONE

Tuesday, November 7th, 2056; 10:12am
Presque Isle, Maine

There are many ideas of war, a few varying definitions and always one cause: control, i.e. power, ownership. Rarely has war been about anything else. What can be said of the soldiers who have fought the battles of the rich for centuries? That answer depends on the type of soldier, doesn't it? You have soldiers who believe with all their heart what they are told by their government. Then there are those who believe in the cause. At last, you have the bloodthirsty soldier who simply needs to take his sociopathic behavior somewhere it would not be frowned upon. I speak as a son of a soldier. I speak as a man that has seen the suffering war has caused and its end results, which only varies if you are the victor or the defeated. Do you enjoy watching children cry, screaming in terror because their parents were killed, or they lost a limb, or they are starving to death, sick, and all the worse, afraid because they feel helpless? Life has got to be about more than this, more than what we can see. Believe me, after what I experienced in my youth, I know now, it is about more. Because I chose it to be that way. Do you have the power of choice? Yes. But do you fully understand the meaning and the uses of this power? Probably not.

My name is Jackson Glass. I have a one-bedroom apartment in downtown Pittsburgh, Pennsylvania. I am a twenty-eight year old freelance investigative reporter. Three weeks ago, News Weekly Magazine contracted me, to do an interview with someone I, frankly, never thought I would ever meet. I was sent to meet with Richard Bridges, the last of the "real" Presidents this country had. I say *real* because he actually had authority in his day, unlike these so-called Presidents today. He has been in prison for some time now and the "mag" wants to do a piece on him. Some say he got a raw deal, some say he got what he deserved for killing all of those people, and then the way he ended the war. Many believe dropping the bomb on China was uncalled for. I can't say it wasn't. I mean isn't that war? Hey, he did what he did and now he has to bite the bullet. Maybe you cannot tell that I don't really want to go in there, I don't want to do this interview. I'd much rather be basking in the sun on the beaches of the Bahamas or the new beaches they recently finished constructing in Miami. It's winter, but there are parts of the world that are still blazing hot right now and I am here in the "great state of Maine", where this "once upon a time" somebody got himself locked up. I heard that the leadership in Russia is undergoing another change that their leader is dying at the age of seventy-two. The Prime Minister of Russia is selecting his successor; I would have liked to have been there, interviewing the man whose war divided the world literally in half.

Okay, I have to get my head together. What are my main objectives for this interview? I had to think this thing through. I am not going to do another "day in the life of" story, no revisiting his glory days, or even rehash the issues of his impeachment. I have to do an article of substance. I need an angle. Something that will stand out for at least a month, something that will make the politicians want to read as well as the pundits. So what do I want from this meeting? What would the readers want to read about, and then talk about the day after they read the article? I have done stories that ruined the careers of three Senators, a governor, and two mayors. I have uncovered the dirt behind some of the most corrupt businesses in New York State when I was a working at my college paper! I am one of the few reporters that Communist governments will allow within their borders. I have been to Syria, Russia, Germany, and Saudi Arabia and came out untouched. My resume is starting to impress even *me*! But here I am. No adventure, no real dirt to dish, just a has-been politician. I just hope I don't fall asleep while he's talking. What is he, like in his sixties by now? Jeez.

I arrived in my 2020 Jupiter model Cessna plane. She is a classic! I call her "Bridget" after my mother. I love that plane; we've been everywhere together. As for my mother, well, she died when I was young but I do remember the times we had together. The conditions of my flight were pretty daunting, as the weather in Maine today did not seem to want to agree with me. I got out of my plane and left Bridget in a hanger at the new Aroostook National Airport in a city called Presque Isle. A car, sent by the News Weekly people, took me the rest of the way. The prison was built at the beginning of the century and is located on the East branch of the Penobscot River, not that far from the national park and Mount Katahdin. The federal government took one hundred and twenty acres of wilderness and turned it into a maximum-security prison to house some of

America's most vicious convicted felons and one former US President. It is a shame that I had to see the beautiful landscape of this state as a prison visitor rather than a tourist. Look at those slopes! I should have brought my skis with me. But then again the snow is coming down really hard, so maybe it worked out for the best.

As I sat in the backseat of a very comfortable classic 2029 Lincoln Town car, I attempted to prepare myself for meeting this... this person, criminal, a former world leader. I used my *Macintosh Pocket PC* and did some research on the Internet and found all I could about Richard Bridges and his family. After forty-five minutes, I have found some basic info like Bridges grew up in a middle class blue-collar type of family, in Houston, Texas. He graduated third in his class at Columbia University in New York and second in his class at Harvard Law School in Boston. This was before the attacks that leveled New York City, of course. He married during his undergrad years. He practiced law until his patriotism got the better of him and he enlisted as an officer in the Air Force and then he was stationed in England, Jordan, and finally Israel where it all went down. He flew his jet over enemy airspace and without orders, bombed the crap out of an encampment of Arabs that were on our side. He claimed that he thought it was an enemy base but no one believed it was an accident, not with America's history for trigger-happy soldiers dating back to Vietnam. I don't know, he has like seven different answers for why he did it, depending on who is asking!

Then I found some not so basic information. A year into his sentence his wife filed for divorce and his kids stopped visiting him a long time ago. It's a shame when you think about it. I mean, America's first African-American President, a man that was decorated for his service and ended World War III, reduced to a black eye on America's face! I don't really know what to think about him. It's not like I know him personally or anything. But then again, I am supposed to remain objective, right? Okay, here we go.

Richard M. Nixon Federal Penitentiary, 12:37pm
As I left the car, I noticed right away, how dismal Nixon Federal Prison seemed. Is that ironic or what? That the prison should be named for a President that should've

went to one, and now it houses one in actuality, is a bit humorous to me. It was a large tan brown facility surrounded by a very high fenced wall. Surrounding the campus was a forest, thick as far as I could see with Mount Katahdin casting its shadow over the prison. With a large river and some lakes, no towns for at least one hundred miles, I wonder if anyone will attempt an escape. Then there is the one stretch paved road I came in on. After a two-hour drive, I had finally reached the gates of this… place. A US Marshall met me at the gate and took me to meet the facility's Warden, one William Atkins. The Warden and I talked for a few minutes; he seemed like a man that was well versed in the art of "small talk". He was tall, probably six feet and three or five inches tall, but quite along around the waist, white guy in his late forties, with a regional accent not familiar to these parts. If I had to guess, I'd say he was from either New Orleans or Mississippi, somewheres around Biloxi. Either way, he had a very thick southern drawl that just didn't sound like Florida or Georgia, not even Texas. He wore a navy blue suit that seemed a little dingy but his shoes, his shoes were black and well polished. His desk was well organized, that kind of thing my mother used to tell me, "a place for everything and everything in its place", yeah that kind of deal.

The Warden and four Marshalls armed to the teeth escorted me to an interrogation room. I was led into a medium sized room; the walls were a grayish kind of blue. The chairs and the table were made of stainless steel. The atmosphere is dreary, depressing, I guess that is how a prison is supposed to feel. I thought it was a bit excessive but the Warden said they were for Bridges' protection as much as they were for ours. While I waited for Bridges to arrive, a call came for me. It was a lawyer from DC, he instructed me on what I can and cannot ask Bridges and of course, what topics I should refrain from discussing and as expected, his disclaimer regarding the consequences to follow, should I choose not to comply with his instructions. He even ordered me to not refer to Bridges as Mr. President, or any other official titles. Who the hell do these people think they are. Some free government. I know how to conduct an interview dammit. The door opened and there he was. He walked in to the room and it felt like he still commanded the respect of his former office. He wore a blue denim jump suit with his last name and ID numbers on the front and back of his shirt. His hands and feet were cuffed and connected by a chain. Richard Bridges, the man. He was around six feet tall, with salt and pepper hair and appeared to be in better shape than myself. His complexion was more of a caramel brown. He came with nothing but his chains and a Bible in his hands.

He quietly sat down when given the order to do so from the Marshall carrying the semi-automatic assault rifle. His face seemed solemn; you just know that this place has done something to him. His pictures from his time on the outside are so different from the man in front of me. He opened his mouth to speak and with what was left of his Texas accent he said to me, "Hello. You are Glass correct? Jack Glass from the *News Weekly Magazine*?" His voice was deep, but friendly. I answered "Y-yes I am. It's a pleasure to meet you. Sorry it had to be under such circumstances." He smirked and said, "Circumstances, yes. This does appear to one of those indeed. I am sure you received instructions about this interview, as I have." I laughed under my breath, "Yes, I sure did. Actually, I got them only a few minutes before you showed up. They sure have good timing, huh?" He said, "It would seem so." I asked him if he was ready to begin and he responded, "Might as well, since I'm here now." I asked him, "Do you mind if I record this? It just helps me to keep my notes and quotes straight." "Let's do it", was all he said back to me.

So I pressed the button on my digital recorder and Bridges said, "That thing sure looks expensive. Does it work well?" I said, "It better work well as much as I paid for it. It's a digital voice recorder and camera in one. I've had this thing since my first major interview with a bigwig member of the City Council back in college. This thing can hear a fly fart." He laughed a little and asked me what school I graduated from, so I told him Buffalo State College. "Oh, you went to a state college. You sure did well for yourself." He said seeming surprised at my education and my reputation, "I was told that you are a rising star among journalists. I don't know how much that really says about you since I personally don't think much of reporters anyway." I replied to him, "Well you know it's not really about *where* you went to school, but what you do with that education in the real world." He smiled and said, "Good. You have a brain. That was a good response. Sorry, I have a habit of sizing up people as I meet them but you did well. Don't worry I feel like you, I believe that the quality of one's education does not differ because of the school's label. I just went to Columbia because I knew that as Black man, I had to bring more to the table if I wanted people to believe in me as a man, lawyer, and a politician. You know, I am starting to like you. You remind me of a friend I once had back in school. He was plucky like you seem. Look, in my time, I have come across so many half twits who attempted to conduct a serious interview and it turned out to feel like a fluff piece instead." "Well, you don't have to worry about me," I said, "We are gonna get down to the *nitty gritty*. Let's begin."

The First Interview:

Glass: Hello Mr. President. I'd like to thank you for allowing this interview.

Bridges: Not at all. It's nice to talk to someone new and get my perspective out to the interested public.

Glass: Good. Good. Okay, let me ask you, what made you decide to join the military when you had a promising career as an Assistant District Attorney for New York State?

Bridges: Well, I don't know if I would call it "promising", I was only a few years out of law school when I was appointed to that position. The Communists were constantly targeting New York City and I was living in Syracuse when the last bomber planes finally demolished the city. I will never forget the way the Statue of Liberty looked on TV, as it slowly crumbled apart, and then fell into the Atlantic Ocean. That was when I knew that I had to do something. This wasn't a "war" like… say Bush's "War on Terrorism", you know? Money had nothing to do with this. I guess that was how the soldiers must have felt when they went into battle during World War II. This war, like that one and the one before it, was about our freedom. Not the freedoms enumerated in the Bill of Rights of the old Constitution, or the freedoms of the new one, but the freedom to simply *be*. The freedom of being free, to not be enslaved or told what to do with your life and having no choices. The absolute basic God-given freedoms we take for granted over and over again.

Glass: Agreed.

Bridges: You know… war is a funny thing. You see it's a tool. A carpenter uses his hammer to pound a nail into a wall; likewise, a government uses war to pound another into submission. The strategies we create seem flawless; we execute them without error. Nevertheless, we neglect to think about the human factor. We neglect to realize that people are going to die when that submarine or Stealth Bomber F-119C lets loose its missiles or that our soldiers' lives are at the same great risk as the enemy's.

Glass: If that is so, then why did you do it? Why did let loose *your* dogs of war on the people of China that night in 2042?

Bridges: Son, those 'dogs of war' were never *mine* to unleash. The loss of life globally, was staggering. Over seventy million people died. The number was just so high. I could not see the war lasting any longer. Then the number went over one hundred million in one night. But the people trusted me, the elected me to end the war--

Glass: (interrupting abruptly) Elected? You say the people elected you to end the war, to be what? Their savior...our savior, or mine? Were you not impeached and convicted of rigging both of your elections? In essence, the two candidates who ran against you won. Correct me if I am wrong sir?

Bridges: Don't die believing every single thing the history books have in them. 'History is written by the victor.'

Glass: Huh, Star Trek. So, you actually watch that? Do they get it in here?

Bridges: Are you kidding? I absolutely love that show. I wish they still aired those re-runs. Listen, the point is there is always three sides to a story: their side, your side and then there is the truth.

Glass: Why did your wife leave you sir?

Bridges: (saying sarcastically) Well, since you asked. She couldn't live with the shame, so opted to disassociate her self from me, ...and my situation. She said she could not take being known as the wife of the only criminal President. I humorously mentioned that most US Presidents were criminals in one-way or another. Washington refused to free the slaves, when he came to power. Lincoln refused to "free" the slaves, if you can recall his main goal was to keep the Union in tact. The first President to be impeached, Andrew Johnson, Congress made laws to set him up, and he fell into it but he was never convicted. Weren't the actions of that Congress illegal?

Glass: What was her response to that?

Bridges: She threw a vase at the wall, said that I always "have to make a joke", and stormed out of the house crying.

Glass: Have you had any contact with her or your children since your incarceration?

Bridges: No. They do not come to see me nor do they call. The last time I heard from my wife was when her lawyer came here to have me sign the divorce papers. What judge wouldn't grant a divorce under these… *circumstances*?

Glass: I am sorry to hear that. If you had it to do all over again, what would you change?

Bridges: *Humph,* I would have gotten *on* that goddamn plane that day. (*He said under his breath*).

Glass: Excuse me? Could you repeat that sir?

Bridges: N-Nothing. Nothing. I was saying that I would not have run for a second term.

Glass: Hmm… I am sorry sir, but I thought I heard say something about a plane. Could you have been referring to the bomber you flew over the Jordan border and used to destroy a camp of civilian insurgents?

Bridges: (angrily responding) I DID NOT KILL THOSE PEOPLE! (Slamming his fists onto the table) DAMMIT! I am not a fool! When I flew on missions, I always did *my* homework. I knew who and where the enemy was! What? Do you think I was incapable of telling a red flag from a Palestine flag waiving in the air in the middle of a desert? I knew they were there; they have been there for months! Damn those traitors in Washington.

The Warden enters and interrupts Bridges. "Calm down Bridges! That's it! This interview is done for today. Glass, call me in the morning and I'll see if you can continue then."

~Interview ended~

I packed up my note pad, got my recorder in my bag. Again, the Marshalls escorted me only this time they walked me to the gate. Once through, I got into the car and headed for my hotel to check in. We drove back to Presque Isle. I did not feel comfortable with staying in a motel in one of the small towns between the prison and the city. Call me paranoid. I stayed at a Howard Johnson's, it wasn't like the Ramada, but it was nice to be out of the cold. My room was a bland beige color, with one single bed, a color TV with the major satellite movie stations, and a small closet that was the size of a coffin.

Before an hour had passed, I had listened to the interview more than once. I was taken aback at how upset he got when I brought up the bombing. My curiosity had been piqued. Why would he respond like that to something he admitted to almost three decades ago? I figured it was late, I'm tired. I'd kick my feet up and wake up to deal with this later. At least I would feel refreshed. I remember putting my head on my pillow at 5:49pm. The time was the last thing I saw, before my eyes closed.

7:35pm

Rrrrring! Rrrrring! Rrrrring! Rrrrring!

I awoke to the sound of my phone ringing loudly, as I reached for the receiver I paused. Who even knows that I am here? I haven't had the chance to tell my editor where I was staying. I picked up the phone and said "Hello?" A man on the other end said, "I don't think you want to upset the President like that again. Now do you Glass?" I said to the voice "uhhh, N-No, not at all. Wait, who is this?" He said to me, "Me? I am someone who knows what happened in that room today. You asked questions that you were previously instructed to avoid. Listen to me, my friend, I would like us to be friends. Because we happen to have a friend in common…" (both saying) "Bridges", "Yes." he said, in a rather smug manner. You know the tone, when you can tell he enjoys knowing something I did not. I do not like Cloak and Dagger type of games, so this was truly vexing me. The voice then told me that I was at the edge of a precipice, that I was bordering one of the most dangerous and most important historical discovery since Kennedy's murderer was revealed to be Linden B. Johnson. He said, "Do you believe everything your elected officials tell you? Can you trust them with your life?" I replied, "I wouldn't be trusting them with my life. I don't know. I have a hard time trusting anyone at this point."

The voice said "There is nothing wrong with that. We live in a world where loyalty is bought and sold like oranges and apples at the grocery store. Listen, what I am about to tell you is the truth. Our mutual friend instructed me to impart this information to you. He feels that you are *trustworthy*. I have my reservations, but I will not question him." I said, "Well then, you better let me have it." Then he said to me, "Not like this. As I have already proven by calling you, the walls have ears, phones have taps, and spies are all around us. Meet me in twenty minutes at the diner on the corner of Seneca Avenue. I will be sitting in a booth, alone. You should come alone as well. Your driver is not one to be trusted; I fear your newspaper may not be his only employer."

I agreed to meet him but when I asked how I would know whom to look for he said, "I know your face, I'll give the brim of my cap a tilt. Look for me." And like that, he hung up. I got dressed quickly and headed down to the lobby of the hotel. I asked the hotel clerk for directions to Seneca Avenue and headed to the diner.

8:06 pm

I arrived at the corner of Seneca Ave; I looked at my watch and realized I was a little late. The red neon light beaming down on me from the diner's sign made a sizzling kind of sound that made it feel like it was frying my brain. I hurried inside to make my meeting and to get out of the light. I walked in and there was a bell over the door that "dinged" upon my entrance. Some people eating their meals and chatting away paused to turn and look my way and then just as quickly, resume their meals and conversations. I walked further into this "greasy spoon", as my dad always called them, and saw mostly couples or a couple of families enjoying their night. That is until I came upon a bearded Caucasian man, dressed in a red flannel shirt, and blue jeans wearing the same black cap as the Marshals back at Nixon Federal Prison with a yellow star right on the front, carefully keeping his head down. He was of slim build but I wouldn't underestimate his fighting ability. Then, as his head rose, his eyes met mine and he tilted the brim of his cap like the voice said.

Without getting up, he said to me with a smirk, "Good evening Mr. Glass" he continued, "took you long enough to get here. What happened?" I looked at him carefully. Naturally, I was suspicious of him; I mean, he is unwilling to tell me his name. He looked like he was in his thirties but that might be because of his well-manicured, grayish beard. I looked him in the eye and said, "Nothing happened. What am I doing here? What does *he* want me to know?" The man looked down at his coffee and began to say, "Years ago, an event in the Middle East was covered up and the truth has since been distorted. Would you like to know the real reason he was convicted for these crimes?" I cannot lie, he had my complete attention, and yes, I did want to know what was beneath what we were told by historians… by the government. "Speak", I said. "Have you called the Warden to schedule your next interview? Once you do that, I will contact you to give you the instructions. We must all appear to be doing exactly what we are supposed to be doing, at all times. If the right people knew I was here with you, we'd both be dead before we got off this street. Now make the call and get some sleep."

And with that said, he got up and walked out of the diner. I went back to my room on foot and made my call.

<u>CHAPTER TWO</u>

Wednesday, November 8th, 2056; 9:00am
En route to Nixon Federal Penitentiary

I don't know why but I don't usually engage in any type of lengthy conversations with my drivers. Well, this morning, in light of what was said last night, I got to know him a little better on the way to Nixon. He relayed to me the following: his name was Carlton Fanning, he has a studio apartment in a small town near Presque Isle but goes where the job tells him to, he is single, no children, and oh yeah, he was ten years my senior. He also mentioned that he was originally from Richmond, Virginia. Well, being who I am, I sat in the backseat, got my computer, and used the info he just gave me and checked him out. All the while, I pretended to play some new computer game on my PC. Within minutes, I pulled up some important particulars on one Carlton Fanning and look there's a picture too! God I love the Internet. I contacted a friend in Philadelphia to do a background check on my new friend Carl, he confirmed that I have correct info except for a few tidbits that I am sure Carl felt were unimportant. Such as, he did a three-year bid in the San Theresa State Prison; an old maximum penitentiary built back in '06 on Isla Mona off the coast of Puerto Rico. The charges were Murder in the 2nd degree and Possession of a Concealed Weapon. Apparently, our guy here was a hired hit and "clipped" someone in San Juan a few years back. It seems that he never really left the business. He's gained the attention of the FBI during his stay here in Maine, linking him to some pretty rugged illegal businessmen. My AP pass gets me everywhere and my friends take me further.

Well, that tells me that I *cannot* trust Carl, but it also means that I *can* begin to trust the bearded fellow from last night. I can't help but wonder what Bridges could be leading me into?

11:40am

I arrived safely to the prison, again, for one more interview with Richard Bridges. Maybe I can get some time alone with the guy and talk to him "privately" or at the very least, what passes for privacy in this place. Upon entering the main building, I was greeted by the Warden in the halls. With his thick accent he said to me, "Good day Mr.

Glass. Let's hope today will be a little more productive." I responded, "Yes, let's hope so." He escorted me to a different location this time, but with the usual entourage in tow. He closed off the cafeteria and said that we could conduct our interview here. I wondered why he chose this place instead of using the room we had yesterday. There were guards at every entrance, in the kitchen, and in the halls surrounding the room.

Bridges entered the room in his usual attire; blue denim overalls, cuffs on hands and feet and the chain. It's as though they are expecting him to make a break for it or something. I don't understand why they fear this "retired" politician who happens to be in his sixties! He greeted me in a manner I now believe is his custom. The same not so chipper, but not so downtrodden, tone of voice and appearance. I am sure that he knows of my meeting last night and yet he behaved as though nothing transpired the night before. We shook hands, nodded our heads, and sat across from each other. I asked him if he was ready for me to start. He said, "Let's begin this", sounding quite irritated. The secret was all I could think as I took out my note pad and clicked on my recorder. I wanted to talk to him about what the bearded man said to me, but I knew I had to contain myself and be patient. In all of my years and experience as a Journalist, in all of my interviews, I have never been so involved, if that is the proper phrase to use here, in such subversive dealings.

The Second Interview:
Glass: Let's start light. What kind of music do you listen to?
Bridges: I grew up on R&B mostly the classics like Aretha Franklin, Patti LaBelle, Diana Ross, then there's R&B from the 90's and the early century artists like Ashanti, Destiny's Child, and Mary J. Blige. I liked Alanis Morrisette, Avril Lavigne too. It's a shame how Avril died; kind of like what happened to Aaliyah, Lisa Lopes, and Ritchie Valens. Umm, by high school I was listening to Hip-Hop artists both current and some oldies.
Glass: What do you believe could have prevented World War III? If you had the power at the turn of the century, what would you have done differently from Bush?

Bridges: Well, first of all, I would have never destroyed the World Trade Center and attacked the Middle East as he did. As we now know, the events of that day, set the stage for WW III. If you asked me this several years ago, I would have given you a different answer, but times have changed, dramatically. The government of today's America is not the one of my youth. George Washington was honored when I was a child, today, the dirty laundry of any President are simply aired out in public as examples of why the old government didn't work. I would have done as Bill Clinton did. I would have removed certain national leaders from office without the world knowing America had a hand in it. Unlike Bush, I would have gotten rid of Saddam Hussein without the U.N., or the American people coming down on me for it. Bush just wasn't fit for the job.

Glass: Today, history tells us George W. Bush actually *did* steal the elections of 2000 and 2004 in the same manner that you were accused of. This forced the Bush family out of the political arena. Records revealed that John F. Kennedy was in fact, executed by those of the old U.S. Government, as high up as Linden B. Johnson; his Vice President. Racism, "classism", and greed prevented men of African descent, to successfully attain the highest office in the country. Allowing *you* to become the first and only Black President in the history of this country only thirty some odd years before the country would have turned three hundred years old! Why not in the 1900's? Korea, Vietnam, the Middle East, Russia, all were wars that could have been prevented, they were unjust and it could have cost the lives of everyone on Earth. With such obviously rampant corruption, why did such a government continue to exist, functioning as a rabid beast attacking and swallowing countries that had resources that fit the government's needs? Why did it take *your* removal to fix the broken machine?

Bridges: Have you ever seen a wealthy man or woman give up their wealth? Only Mother Theresa. In your studies, did you read of any one Roman Emperor renounce his throne? So, it was that no one would ever see American Imperialism end until it finally collapsed on its own. Really, it was a matter of time before that government fell. But no one ever thought it would have been like this. Abraham Lincoln was the Civil War president. He had to find a way to keep the Union intact. His main concern was not slavery. It was all about America becoming the great industrial country it eventually became in the 20th Century. Think of America as a plate, spinning atop a tall stick. It would only need to be tapped, just a little, for it to tip over, fall and break into pieces. The new Congress kept the Union intact when I was removed, when states tried to break away and form new countries, good on them. They kept it together in light of my embarrassment. Then, there were those within the Legislative branch who have been looking for ways to bring down the government, seize the powers of the President thereby increasing their own, making them virtually untouchable. More powerful than a President and the people bought it. I was charged, tried, judged, and politically and personally executed. My life, as I knew it, was over. No family, no friends, no freedom, no type of hope. My enemies in Congress took my life and weren't even decent enough to actually kill me.

Glass: What do you mean by that?

Bridges: Don't you think it was a little curious how I could rig a Presidential Election in 54 states? Or that my public opinion ratings were higher than Ronald Reagan or George W. Bush or even Franklin Delano Roosevelt and in an instant, a single document ended my career. A classified document mind you, was released all over the Internet saying that I killed nearly a hundred Arabs civilian troops, fighting against their Communist rulers? There are people that hold seats in the Congressional Houses that once served with me during that very incident. Where were my witnesses? Who was there to corroborate my story? I felt like Lee Harvey Oswald, screaming "I'm just a damn patsy". The Congress wanted control. This Congress realized their predecessor's greatest dreams.

Glass: What are you saying?

Bridges: You are a smart boy; I think you can figure it out. I am done here. Good day to you Mr. Glass. (Whispering to Glass) I'll be seeing you in the future.

~Interview Ended~

"Wait! You can't go yet." I said to him. Suddenly, he rushed toward me and said in my ear, "You know what you need to know. I will tell you more, not now, not here!" Two guards grabbed him by his arms and pulled him away from me.

I left the premises and got into the backseat of the car waiting for me. We drove for half an hour when my driver and I noticed a man in a dark over coat and hat stood in the middle of the road and seemed to be flagging us down. Carl, the driver, asked me what I wanted to do. When I saw the man's face, I insisted that Carl stop the car and pick him up. Carl asserted that it wouldn't be wise to pick up hitchhikers. I told him it was okay. He pulled the car to side of the road and the man got in the back seat and sat next to me. He said, "How are you today sir. My name is Knight, Elijah Knight. Thanks for pulling over. I am headed to Presque Isle, is that on your way?" I looked at him, wondering why he was pretending not to know me, and then I realized it was for Carl's benefit. I asked Carl if he could put the partition up so that I may speak in private to my guest. So he did.

Knight said to me in a low voice, "With what you heard back there, you are in greater danger. Remember, I told you to trust no one. There are those who work within that facility who report directly to the US Senate and its President." I asked him "Can you tell me what is going on here? What are you guys getting me into?" He said, "Some years ago, the Senate secretly authorized the release of classified documents that named Bridges as the pilot of the bomber jet that killed those Arab civilian soldiers. They were organizing the impeachment process before the election scandal came out. Between the that document's presentation and the impeachment of Bridges, documents that could have exonerated him were destroyed while others to condemn him were forged, his witnesses were sent abroad or murdered. There are a few left that know the truth; most of them sit in the Senate and on the US Supreme Court, his case was resided over by Chief Justice Starks, a friend and supporter of Senator Hames.

Bridges did not fly that jet, and he was legally elected President, both times. There are documents hidden within the Pentagon that will reveal to you the truth. You must take this envelope; it has a layout of the building directing you were to go to find the information." I couldn't help feeling a pressing need to preserve my own life and asked Knight, "Why me? Why do I have to go there?" His only response to that question was, "You my friend were chosen. Your father was one of those who served with the

President in Israel that day. He knew the truth and was more than willing to speak on Bridges' behalf. How did your dad die?" Without even thinking, I said, "He died of a heart attack while vacationing in St. Thomas."

"My poor boy. There exists a group that acts as enforcers for the US Senate, a group originally instituted by Richard Nixon to plug "leaks", known as the "Plumbers". They never went away, just because "Tricky Dick" did. The Plumbers are a band of ex-cons from various South American countries that have come under Communism. A vicious killer, a man known only as "Trini", leads them. He escaped life imprisonment in Colombia by killing his captors; he then chopped off their hand to use for DNA scanning and made it to a ship sailing for Mexico. You see him I don't care what you may think, you run. He is a well-trained assassin and loves hand to hand combat. They caught your father in Jordan, searching for a man named Edgar T. Moses, a former Naval Captain who took early retirement by abandoning his post upon discovering the cover up that almost got Bridges court-martialed."

"Moses went across the border into Communist Jordan with a case of 'Thumb Drives'. These are small hard drives, no bigger than your index finger, designed to hold 120 gigabytes of data that to this day, hold incredibly sensitive information that could bring down certain members of the current Senate. Hundreds of bytes of info regarding their secret activities and covert dealings with the Communist Party. And one file that contains the truth about who flew that jet, the day Bridges was supposed to have piloted it, and why they destroyed the camp. Days after your father located Moses, the Plumbers got a hold of your dad and strangled him to death. Later on, we purposefully sent Moses copies of vital documents containing information regarding the election fiasco after Bridges was convicted, scrambling the signal from the point of origin to its final destination for safekeeping. Unfortunately, the original documents are no longer stored at the Pentagon. Moses is the only one with that info now. He broke contact with us a while back but we have good intelligence suggesting he is still alive and that left Jordan some years ago. Currently, he is residing in the mountainous region of Tajikistan, in a city called Murghob. That's where I will be going, but you have a different mission."

Amazed, I asked him, "H-how can you know all of this? How can I know this is the truth?" He told me, "This Marshall thing is just a cover to keep me close to Bridges. I am a high ranking agent of the CIA---" "But," I interrupted, "they were dissolved when the new Constitution was set in place." "No, we became the agency that operated quietly throughout the world, putting in place the players the Senate selects to maintain their hold on the remaining free world and to one day overthrow the Communist Alliance, permanently. All of our documents, files, even our agents are headquartered in the bowels of the Pentagon." He continued, "Take these with you; it will help you to get in without being discovered." He handed me a large manila envelope with his ID card, badge, and other documents, all labeled, "C.I.A." in big blue letters at the top, each page had security access codes to get me in and out safely. So, the government had my father killed? This was too much to take in all in this small amount of time! I mean, I just found out my dad didn't die the way I was told. I felt my anger grow within me and my heart pounded heavily in my chest. I knew from this day on, my life would be different.

Back at Nixon Federal Penitentiary; at the same time.

In the office of the Warden, Atkins received a phone call. "Yes sir. I know for a fact, they were both instructed to stay away from certain topics. But I think it goes deeper than a simple breech of agreement, I think Bridges may be trying to lead Glass into helping his cause." said Atkins. The voice over the phone said, "Well then… for safety sake, I think it's time to remove Mr. Glass in a manner that will not raise suspicion. The last thing we need is a scandal of any sort. We are in a tough enough position to solidify this agreement with the Communists. No one need know that Glass has vanished be cause of us. Am I clear Atkins? Handle this problem with care but effectively."

"Yes, yes I understand sir. B-but what am I to do about Bridges?" Atkins asks the voice. "Do not worry yourself with that problem. We will decide when the time is right to deal with him." With a click, he hung up and the voice was gone. Atkins dialed a cell phone number written in his *At-A-Glance* digital directory and pulls up a name and number, which he dials quickly. "I want you to get rid of Glass now." Atkins orders the man on the other end of the phone. The man responds, "Fine, but he has company right now. We just picked up a stray on the road." "What?! Who is it?" Atkins asks. "I dunno who he is but he feels like an agent. I can guarantee it. What do you want me to do?" Atkins said, "Solve the problem quickly and quietly. Eliminate them." The man replied, "Understood. Out."

Resuming the conversation between Glass and Knight in the car.

"Do you understand what you have been told Glass? Bridges needs you; this country needs you. At the same time that the Senate is trying to rebuild this country, they are tearing it apart and selling out its citizens with every day that passes. Every one in North America is in grave danger. We have reason to believe, the senate will deliver a surrender to the Communist Party, and as a part of the deal, certain individuals will gain powerful positions while the rest of us fall under them. America will be no more. You must provide us the information that will crush Senate President Edward Hames and clear Bridges of his so-called crimes. Once the people know what is going on, Hames and his people will be out!" The only words that I could push passed my lips were "WHY ME? Why don't you do it? I am not trained in espionage. I am not a spy. I am a reporter." Knight responded, "I am too high profile. But my authorization will get you where you need to go. They are going to kill you regardless of your involvement after what happened back at the prison. So how do you want to go out? Fighting or whining?"

All of a sudden, the car comes to a screeching halt. Soon after, we heard the front door open and close. It appeared to us that Carl got out and left us. But why? In an instant, gunshots were fired at the Knight's side of the car. He said, "What are you waiting for? Get the hell out!" So I did. I ran into the thicket bordering the surrounding forest and hid there while Knight followed me in, shooting back at our assailant. Knight ran up to me and said, "Listen, we *have* to make it out of here alive. Do you understand what I am saying to you Glass? We have to kill him. Here, have you ever fired a pistol before?" I told him the truth, "Yeah, my dad taught me." He said, "Okay good, just pretend that he is one of those pieces of paper with a target on him and shoot. Go to the front of the car and I'll go around the back. On my order... we'll rush the S.O.B. from either side and nail him." "Alright!" I said with adrenaline raging through my bloodstream. Then all I heard was "GO!" We followed the plan and I fired my gun right at the spot I heard Carl's gunfire coming from. Then, as Knight ran toward the trees on the left side of Carl, I did the same, only I went right. Of course.

I had it set in my mind that today: I was going to kill a man. Once I made it under the cover of a White Pine tree, things went quiet. Then I heard the rustling of branches and crunching of dried leaves. The noises were getting louder, like it was coming my way. Once it was close enough, I jumped in front of the oncoming noise and aimed my gun at him; it was Carl. "What the hell, are you doing Carl?" I shouted to him. He said "This my job. You have yours and I have mine. Listen kid, it's not like it was personal. I have nothing against you." And, in what felt like an eternity but could have only been an instant, he raised his arm toward me and fired three shots. My eyes shut closed. In that instant, Knight jumped right in front of me, from out of nowhere and fired back. From my angle, I saw the bullets Knight let off hit Carl in the neck and face. Then Knight dropped to the dirt right in front of me. I squatted down to him and with labored breath, he said to me, "You have to take what I have given you…I can't…help you anymore. Stop them. Stop Hames, before we fall… to our… enemies. I promise kid... Hitler will seem like nothing if …they get control." Then he stopped speaking, his eyes were still, they were open, and then it was completely quiet. He was gone. His blood was everywhere, including on my clothes and hands. This is not the first time I saw a dead body, but it was the first time I watched someone die. He died… saving me.

I heard Carl over there, still breathing. The shots got him on the right side of his neck, one went through his cheek, and another tore off his left ear. He was breathing hard. I guess he could feel his life leaving him as his blood spurted from his neck. It must have hit an artery; he'll be dead very soon was all I knew. He said with as much energy as he could muster, "You will be dead soon too. Nothing you do will change anything." I felt in my heart that he was wrong and I needed to prove it to him. I stood over him, looking down at him I could see he had no fear of dying. I cocked my gun and aimed it at his forehead. I said to him, "Things will change." I inhaled deep and fired my weapon. As the loud bang of the gun went off, I raised my head, looking away, and I could see birds flying from the trees into the white cloud filled sky. There was nothing more I could do for Knight, I left him were he lay, where no one could see him from their passing car. I felt like I wronged him because I could not help him. I'll make it up to him, I will take up this mission. I looked around to figure out my next move and saw that beautiful, classic automobile riddled with bullet holes. I picked up all of the guns and took them with me, just in case. With little if any options available to me, I got in the shot up car to take me as close as I could get to Presque Isle. Then I could ditch the car somewhere and figure where to go from there. Yeah, that is what I will do.

CHAPTER THREE

Wednesday, November 8th, 2056; 3:13pm
Howard Johnson hotel room 412, Presque Isle, Maine

"Look, I will make this short." Bridges said over the phone, "I am sending someone to meet with you. You can trust her. I was sorry to hear about our friend but the mission must be completed. She will relay all of my directives. Glass, thank you for doing this." I hung up the phone. I put my head on my pillow and replayed the days' events in my mind. Today, a man gave his life for mine; today, I took a life in revenge, and today just doesn't seem to want to end. I just found out that, essentially, the American government, as it was once known to the world, was over thrown and replaced by a new regime. What a day! My phone rang again; it was the lobby telling me I had a guest waiting for me down there. I told him to send her up. I put the "hardware" in my duffle bag and tucked it under the bed. Then there was a knock at my door. I looked through the peephole and saw a woman who had looks that were very pleasing to the eye. I opened the door and she walked in. She was a very light-skinned Black woman, with brown hair and tan colored highlights that flowed down to her shoulders. She must've been about 5'9" or 10", give or take a few. She had a slim, but visibly firm build and I had to check out her figure. Well, she wore a form-fitting suit that had me I completely interested.

She introduced herself as only "Q" and put her hand out for me to shake it. I told her, "I hope you don't mind, but I don't think I'll be shaking hands anymore. It's not you, its just… people." I continued, "Listen, you wouldn't mind waiting for me, would you? I have to take a shower. Maybe, umm… you could watch a little TV. This day is just going so fast, so much happening so quickly, you know. I just have to wash the day off me." Q said, "I don't mind but please remember, we have a schedule to keep to. So, don't turn into a prune in there. Okay?" I nodded my head and jumped in the shower, letting the warm water to run all over my body. In twenty minutes, the therapeutic effects of a hot shower did its job on me and I came out of the bathroom in my towel to find Q sitting in the chair watching the tube. I grabbed some clothes and went back in the bathroom to get dressed.

Q and I got into her car and headed back to the prison. With Bridges calling me like he did, it set my mind at ease, just a little. Knight's words to me about trusting no one still rang in my head every time I saw a new face, and some that were familiar. There was a dead silence in the car as we drove through the mountains; I asked my escort "So what does 'Q' stand for?" Keeping her eyes focused on the road she responded, "Question, Quality, Qualified, or maybe Quandary. Take your pick." By her attitude, I could see that she wasn't in the mood for conversation. Since we met, she seemed unyielding; no question I asked of her was answered to my satisfaction. I made attempts at humor but of course, they were shot down as though Q lacked a funny bone.

Nixon Federal Prison, 5:42pm

Q walked me passed the gated prison entrance, but before we could enter the building, a Marshall appeared and motioned us to follow him. Q's only response was a brief nod in agreement and we proceeded to walk around the main building toward the back way. We walked through a series of tunnels under the prison building, until we came to a door that was engulfed by darkness, with a dim light seeping from behind the hinges. I passed through the threshold of the door, to find a medium sized room filled with steam coming from numerous pipes running along the ceiling. Needless to say, it was quite hot in there. The door was closed behind me and suddenly my guard was up. Weaponless and unable to see clearly, I went into my pocket and pulled out my Uniball pen, yeah, the one with the very sharp tip.

All of a sudden, a hand reached out from behind me and touched my shoulder. Quickly, I turned around with my improvised weapon, ready for use. I got it as close as the figure's throat when I realized it was Bridges. "Whoa, junior!" Bridges exclaimed, "Take it easy buddy. I am sorry that I startled; you but I needed to speak to you somewhere private and this is one of the few locations on the prison campus where no one will hear us." I asked him very simply, "How did you get out of your cell without the guards knowing?" He said, "I have many, many loyal friends within the government and some of them are here tonight ensuring our privacy and our security." "Who? The CIA", I said sarcastically. He retorted "Some. Then there are U.S. Marshalls, FBI, DOD, and

ATF. I have friends at the Pentagon too. That is where you will have to go in order to piece the evidence in this puzzle, together." Then, he had me wondering how in the world am I supposed to get into CIA headquarters and back out alive. I said to him, "So what are you going to do? Give me a cape that will let me pass through undetected like those old Harry Potter movies?" He laughed a little and said "No. I don't have anything to give you to help you in this mission. All that you need, Knight gave to you before he died."

Of course, Bridges was referring to the envelope that had Knight's ID badges and security codes. I can't believe the CIA is still in operation, even though it's illegal for them to exist. "I have to ask you something first." I stated. He said, "Okay, shoot." "Alright… why was I not told earlier about my father's death and why is the CIA still in operation?" "Well Jack, I hope you don't mind me calling you Jack. I mean we are going beyond formalities at this stage, at least I think so. Here it is. We had to be sure, of where your loyalties lie before we could include you in our maneuver to overthrow the current government. Your father was a good friend to me. He saved my life almost as many times as I have saved his." Bridges went on, "We promised to protect each other when the bullets began to rain on us and we kept that promise throughout. You have never served, I know. But you need to understand that when two men make such a promise on the battlefield, it is not one that is broken lightly. He knew that I would have done the same for him. It's a brotherhood and nothing can come between brothers. I stand here now with you and as God as my witness, I will make the same promise to you. I will not allow harm to befall you so long as I am breathing. We can make it through this. Are you with me, Jack?"

I stood there, thinking about what I am getting myself into and why. Their enemies took my dad from me. The people of America had no clue that a coup had taken place when Bridges was impeached. And the Senate grows stronger every day finding new ways to increase their authority; searching for ways to bring wealth to themselves but misery to the rest of us. Communism. What could the senate believe that the Russians would promise them?

My father… I was so young when he died. As was Knight, and I promised to make his death matter. With that thought, I put my hand out and Bridges clasped his hand around mine. "It's a deal. Don't let me down and I will try not to let you down. But from here on in, I want the absolute truth." I said, most assuredly. "Fair deal, son." He said with a smile on his face, pleased I am sure, knowing that I will carry on his quest for "justice". "Now, you wanted to know why the CIA is still around. The President of the Senate decided that it would be in his best interest to keep them operating out the Pentagon and closed down the Langley campus for appearances. You see, when it was revealed, years ago, that the Directors of the CIA conspired to oust George Bush, allowing him to go through with his plans to execute the events of 9-11, the people demanded blood. Relatives of those survivors from that day were still seeking justice. So, Hames gave them the CIA as a sacrificial lamb, laying the blame on no one else, revealing no further information regarding the attacks. But he knew it would be foolish to lose such an efficient asset. So they became an underground operation, doing only the President's bidding."

I jumped in and said, "You mean Todd, the President in charge of Domestic Affairs?" "No." he said to me, "Edward King Hames, the President of the United States Senate and the only real power in this country. He has the dirt on every one holding a political office and some of the wealthiest men and women in this country, as well as in others. The Congress, the Executive branch, they only function as a decoration similar to English monarchs, he runs things now. Soon, everything these people hold in trust will be gone. We are talking about basic civil rights. Forget about the stupid things like online pornography or racism. I mean your ability to choose will soon become a thing of the past. Your right to choose will vanish. I never thought Hames could achieve this but when he was elected to the Senate, I knew it was a matter of time. We would sit around fires, my fellow soldiers and I, in the deserts camps near the Egyptian border. We would talk about all sorts of things. On one of those nights, we sat there, smoking our Dominican cigars and he told me what his ideas of power were. He told me of his plan to get a hold of it. Then he was discharged and became a senator in 2030. Power is all that matters to him. His family is for show. I did not know that he had so many people in his pocket. I underestimated Senator Hames." Bridges said with remorse evident in his tone, "That was my fault. I let my country down and I have to set it right. I am not looking to get my office back, but I do want that son a bitch to pay for what he did to me, what he's done to my life! He has to pay for what he has done to all Americans. We have to stop him from selling the people out for his own personal gain."

I could feel his anger through the tone of his voice. I knew that this was bigger than I thought before. "So what do I do now?" I asked Bridges. "Q will escort you as far as Presque Isle where you will board your plane and get down to Arlington, Virginia. You must not be detected. That plane of yours isn't modern, so you will need to fly low enough to avoid radars. Use the badges and codes to get in, get the Air Force Mission Patrol reports from October 26th -December 19th, 2032 and all files related to it. Copy them the best you can and get the hell out before you are made. Clear? Then you will meet with my man on the outside and we will expose those bastards to daylight." "Are you sure I can do this Bridges? I don't have special training, only what my dad taught me in my youth. I am still trying to soak in that I killed a man today!" "Son, listen to me. You will do just fine. All you have to do is bring those files to me. I will not let you down. I will guide you every step of the way. All right? You'll do well my boy. You are your father's son; the training he gave you is what you will need. So, remember it when it is needed. Now, go… and Godspeed."

Almost as if on cue, here came Q (no pun intended) snatching me by my arm saying, "We have to go. Bridges cannot be away from his cell for too long, it will raise suspicion. Let's get to the car. Do you have everything you need?" I answered, "No. We have to stop at the hotel first, then I will be ready." We hurried out of the tunnels and back under the veil of the dark sky outside. We sped away in Q's car and made it to Presque Isle without a problem.

Presque Isle, 10:08pm

I packed my belongings as quick as I could. After checking the guns I now have possession of, I figured I better get more bullets, just in case. I got my bags and things and ran downstairs to Q. I checked out of the hotel and got into her car waiting right outside. I suggested that we find a gun shop here in town before I left. Q decided against that idea and drove into a parking lot after getting only a few blocks away from the hotel. She parked the car and said, "Give me the gun." I handed here all three and she examined them under the roof light. "Did you think such a store would be open at this hour? Wait… where did you get these?" she said looking at me as though it were peculiar. I told her about what happened this morning. She said, "Okay. Then we have a problem," as she began to reload them. I said "And that would be?" "All of these weapons are CIA standard issue firearms. These three guns are all Artemis .121 semi-automatic handguns made for agents by Rivers Steele, an arms manufacturing company, under secret contract with the Senate. See the Silver bow and arrow on the grip? That tells me that Carl was either armed by one of us or he was one of us."

Thinking aloud I said, "That means what? The CIA is on to me? No. It's more than that. Carl was planted in our midst in order to kill me, from the beginning. He must have been waiting for his orders to do it." "Here", Q said as she handed me back my artillery fully loaded, "You will need these so be careful. You do know how to shoot right?" I said, "Of course I do. My father taught me years ago, and I have been frequenting the firing range in my area to practice over the years. It can be calming when I feel stressed or pissed off." We resumed driving toward our destination, the airport. Just before we arrived, however, Q decided it would be best to lose the car at this point. She drove into a parking garage. We got out with our necessities and left it sitting there. All she said to me was "It wasn't mine anyway." I responded, "What? Was it stolen or borrowed?" "Borrowed, I'd say. I mean, I did give it back, didn't I?" she said chuckling a little, but just a little.

Aroostook National Airport, 11:31pm

We arrived at the airport and Q left me to make my required arrangements before we could take off. She sat in the lounge area of the terminal and got us some grub from King Burger. I don't really make a habit of eating fast food, but I have hardly eaten at all today so hey, if not, why not? You know. "Listen to me," Q whispered to me, "We are going to have to leave soon. We have to get on that plane and get this thing going. What's our ETA in Virginia?" I said, "Well, the weather has let up a bit, the snow isn't falling as heavy as when I arrived, so barring any storm systems developing while we are in the air or any other problems, we should be there within three to four hours. Wait a minute, are you coming with me?" "Of course I am. We can't just send you into the deep end of the ocean without a lifesaver, at least." Q said. "They are fueling the plane for me as we speak…", before she could jump in with concern, I said, "Don't worry, I always inspect the plane inside and out before I take off. So, if anyone *is* trying anything, I will find it before we are in the air, okay. I can't go in there and stand over them, it will look too weird. That kind of behavior is irregular for pilots of small planes, who are supposed to be simple reporters. It would tip them off to my leaving."

After I was notified that the fueling was done and the plane was cleared by their standards, I checked it myself, thoroughly I might add. I asked Q to check for any objects that seemed, out of place on the hull. After we finished, I gave it a once over just for safety sake and found nothing out of the ordinary. By midnight, we had the plane loaded with our bags and we were under way.

CHAPTER FOUR

Thursday, November 9th, 2056; 3:52am
Washington National Airport, Arlington, Virginia

Within a matter of hours, we arrived in Arlington without incident. We rented a car to take us the rest of the way. Q specifically requested a black Ford Orion XS point five, an "All Utility Vehicle" with tinted windows. She said, "You never know what is going to happen, do you?" I just chuckled it off; I was falling apart from exhaustion, so Q drove into Arlington. I asked her, "Q, don't you ever sleep? We've been up for a while now and you don't seem to be the least bit tired like me." She responded, "I sleep when I need to. Fortunately, I already got my sleep, so go ahead and get your rest. You got us this far, I've got it from here." So I did.

Downtown Arlington; 5:57am

When I awoke the sun was just rising in the eastern sky, it was very stunning. The colors of the night sky seemed to be chased away by the dawns' fiery hues blazing across the horizon. The streets were covered in white snow, as were building rooftops. I looked around and noticed Q was not in the driver's seat. I looked for her outside, where I found Q talking on her cell phone; to whom I did not know. She turned around and saw me staring at her. She gave me no reaction except for turning back around. I was looking about the street when I noticed a sign directing toward the Interstate highway toward D.C. There was another sign that read "Welcome to Downtown Arlington", looking at the map, I saw that we completely passed the Pentagon. So why are we here? Q headed back to the car, so I folded the map up and put it back. As she buckled herself in, I proceeded to inquire why we were here and not at the Pentagon. She said, "Sorry, I didn't get your permission first, but I had to hit the head, is that okay with you? If it's alright with you, I'd like to get some breakfast." I said, "Food? Yeah, good idea." We began to drive off when I asked her "So, care to share with me who you were talking to on the phone back there?" All she said was "Our contact on the inside."

We stopped at a McDonald's and I ordered my usual breakfast: eggs with cheese on a biscuit, orange juice and hash browns. Q had coffee, eggs, and sausage on a biscuit and ate it rather quickly. She turned to me as I ate my breakfast, and said "Listen, I know you are trying to make sense of this whole thing, but I know what I am doing. You just have to trust me. If we go in there outside of normal business hours, your ID will do nothing but get their attention. You cannot just break-in to the Pentagon. This isn't some house in Beverly Hills where they have a simple house alarm. The Pentagon has video surveillance everyday, all day. Between 6pm and 8am, they are monitoring everyone and anyone in the building, on the grounds and flying near their airspace. So, let's be the proverbial "needle in the haystack". We'll go in with everyone else at 8:30am. You have Knight's ID and I have my own. We'll get in, make copies of the documents and get the hell out of there before we get killed." I said, "That sounds like a plan to me. I need to get dressed." Q said, "Well, you could change in the bathroom. I got you a suit; it's hanging in the back seat along with the shoes." I said, "Yeah, change and shave, and freshen up a bit. I hope this thing will fit." She said, "Just remember you need to look and act like an agent or the game is over." I shaved my five o'clock shadow, my mustache and dressed in what I assumed to be standard attire for a secret agent of a secret organization that is not supposed to even exist. I combed my hair with a part on the right. It was funny to me because my dad would love to see me now. I always hated dressing up and he didn't understand the feeling.

The Pentagon; 8:33am

We walked into the building lobby, where I saw long lines of people swiping their badges through a reader to get that little green light allowing them entry to the building. Q followed me behind two other people, I did what she said, and I kept my face low to avoid the cameras. I avoided looking too many people in they eye, as they would have been studying my face. I had to behave like a ghost among people, passing through without being touched. After five minutes of standing on line, it was now my turn. I swiped Knight's badge through and at first, the light was red and it beeped. The Security Guard asked me to try again, so I did. This time, I said a quick prayer in my mind and inhaled deeply while trying not to appear nervous or show what I was actually feeling, scared. I swiped it through and it was green. I exhaled my fears away and walked through as the guard said, "Good day, Mr. Knight." I nodded in the guard's direction and headed toward the elevator, Q came through without a hitch. As people tried to get on the elevator with us, Q instructed them to catch another one saying, "Sorry, we've reached occupancy limits, you're going to have to find another elevator guys. Sorry, again." She seems to have fun when she lies.

Q simultaneously pressed the buttons for the basement labeled "B" and the ground floor button labeled "G". The elevator went directly to a level of the building I am sure many of those employed are unaware existed. All of a sudden, she got close to me and whispered, "Don't say anything, they can hear and see us." The elevator stopped and we were closer to our destination. We got off the elevator and began to walk toward the staircase. I asked Q why were using the stairs, she said, "This is the only staircase in the entire building that is not monitored. It's the CIA Director's entrance. I can get us passed the safeguards here and we can get to the Archive room in less than a minute." We reached the door, where I noticed a wall panel that spoke in a computerized female's voice, "Please prepare for retinal scan." Q dug into her inner jacket pocket and pulled out a small case containing contact lenses. She placed them in her eyes, which turned from deep brown to sky blue. She positioned herself directly in front of the scanner. The readout was positive and we were granted entry to the floor. She turned to me and said, "Come on hazel eyes, we don't have a lot of time before the Director arrives.

Office of the President of the U.S. Senate, Edward King Hames
Capitol Hill, Washington D.C.; 9:05am

Sitting behind a large stunning oak desk is Ed Hames. He was a tall, older fellow with a slender build, wearing a very expensive looking dark colored suit, smoking a hand-rolled Dominican cigar. He is a very self-pleasing man, believing that he's the only person in the country worthy enough to wield the power he captured under the guise of protecting the American populace. Hames organized a meeting with members of the Plumbers and the Director of the CIA, Ronald Harris. Hames said to his henchmen, "I am going to make this as clear as possible and I don't want any mistakes. I want efficiency, achievement, and more importantly finality. I want you to locate one, Jackson Glass and bring him to me. Bridges has been a pain in my ass since his wife left him rotting behind those bars in Maine. I'll let you all in on a little secret: I planted several agents among Bridges' supporters who provide me with intelligence regarding their plans and operations. I received reliable information that at this very moment, gentlemen, Glass, and his current partner in crime are attempting to break and enter *your* office, Mr. Harris. Through my agent, we know that his mission is to obtain mission reports regarding the attack on that Arab militia back in '32."

"Those documents are located further in the facility though. How can they get passed our security?" Harris asked Hames. "Well, it appears that he was given security clearance by an agent of *yours* who became a turncoat for Bridges' side. I want this understood by all of you, Glass is not to be harmed. If you kill him, it could cause problems for me. And we don't want that, right? Glass is a well-known journalist; he can't vanish unexpectedly. In Maine it was alright, but now that he's been with Bridges, my enemies who lay in wait might be armed against me should Glass meet an unexpected and bloody death shown all over the news. Okay? I will decide what to do with him later. In addition," Hames continued, "I want those documents destroyed, I want all outside of essential personnel who know about them to disappear, completely and quietly. Hold on," he says reaching for his intercom button, "Lisa?" "Yes, Mr. Hames?" his secretary responds. "I need you to call Rick Graves; he's an Assistant Director over at the Bureau. Tell him that I have yet to receive the email I requested yesterday and have him send it to me in fifteen minutes or less. Got it Lisa?" "Yes sir, Mr. Hames would like me to also order your usual breakfast?" she asks. "As a matter of fact, yes I would. Can you believe I forgot the most important meal of the day!" he says laughingly.

"I have Graves compiling all of the data we have on Glass, his finances, his family, sexual indiscretions, bills; hell what ever else that we may be able to use." Hames continued, "They are in the Pentagon right now. Before he leaves the building, Trini, take your boys, and bring Glass to me. Clear? You are dismissed." "Yes, Mr. Hames." Trini said as he signals his men to leave. "Director," Hames said, "please stick around, we need to talk."

"Yes Mr. Hames." Harris responds. The men known only as "The Plumbers" leave to carry out their orders. "Ronnie..." Hames said speaking to Harris, "what the hell is going on over there? How could you possibly have created such a situation within your agency? I kept the CIA alive in order to fulfill its purpose serving *us*, the Senate, more over, serve me! How could you allow your people to betray us and live to wreak such havoc?" Harris says, "Mr. Hames, if I may speak frankly sir, I minimized security around my office to allow intruders to make such attempts. The computer mainframe records all entries and exits through my office. Anyone who is able to get through them I would like to know who they are so I can have their ass!" "I see. It's a set up." Hames observes, "Clever man, yes, yes. Since you are obviously clever, maybe you can explain the traitors who walk among us then. Why are they still active?"

Harris stands up and walks around his chair and leans in saying, "Sir. I had one of them removed just yesterday at the cost of well-trained and loyal man. He was an ex-con that proved to be a valuable asset to our interests. He has carried out many missions to completion. Until yesterday morning, when a senior agent named Elijah Knight executed him; Glass also aided Knight. Trust me, this has gone beyond government business this is personal for me sir." Hames asked Harris, "The agent killed, you trained him yourself?" Harris answers, "Sir, I trained them both. I simply had no idea that Knight was loyal to Bridges."

"And what of Knight? Do we have his whereabouts?" Hames asked. "Both agents were terminated in that operation, sir." Harris responds, "Only Glass remains. If he made it to my doorstep, it is because he has help. Someone who has the ability to make it passed my security measures. It has to be another top level agent." Hames rose from his seat and walks over to the window, looking at the White House with one hand clasping the other behind his back. Hames said, "That's the thing, Harris. He does have help. This agent is one of your best. I sent this one in personally, sorry I left you of the loop like that but I had to. Everything must have the right feel, the right appearance. It must be completely believable for the ruse to succeed. She is with him as we speak, guiding him into my hands. All you have to do is, not get in the way and make sure none of your boys do either. The country cannot know that the CIA is still in operation, nor can Bridges' secrets be revealed. Your main concern now is the termination of all who are known to be or even suspected of being traitors, collaborators, and conspirators within the agency. My friend, it's time to clean house."

Back at the Pentagon; 10:35am

It took a little while, but I eventually found the exact mission report in question. The security pass codes required were no problem, thanks to Knight. I sent the files to print and took one of their waterproof envelopes to protect the document. Q stayed outside the door to keep agents off my ass while I get this done. I don't know why, but I got this feeling like I might need to have added insurance, just in case something goes wrong. So, I took out my camera/recorder and took digital photos of each sheet of paper. I gave my signal for Q to return, but she didn't. I went to see if I could find her, but first, I removed the "digi-chip" (the camera's memory storage) and placed the chip into a little compartment on the underside of my watch. Something I had built in to the watch when I bought three years ago. I always knew that would come in handy. I've only used it once before when I was on a photo shoot at the edge of the Sahara desert.

Okay, here we go. I slipped out of the office and searched around to see if I could find Q, but there was no trace of her. I didn't know what to think, but my dad's suspicious nature slipped into my consciousness. I began to ask myself, why was Q on that phone earlier? Why is she not here now? Could she be setting me up? To hell with it, she works here she knows her own way out. I headed for the door we entered through and couldn't get it to open without the retinal scan. I looked through Knight's envelope; finally, after searching through several pages, I found one with the words "Director's Security Access" highlighted. I entered the correct code, but then an alarm began beeping. The screen read, "Intruder Alert". They must have been on to Knight and gave him codes that would trigger their security system.

Quickly, I backed up a bit to get a running start and I rammed my shoulder into the door. A door that I thought was steel, but was really glass and I went right through, shattering it to pieces. I landed on the floor next to the staircase. I got up, finding no blood on the floor, I ran up the stairs to make it to the elevator. As I exited the staircase, I heard the footsteps coming after me. I ran to the elevator and hit the button. It lit up but the doors did not open yet! I saw two agents coming out of the staircase and they saw me right in the open. As they darted toward me, I repeatedly hit the button. Once the doors opened, I ran inside and pressed the 'door close' button. As the doors finally closed, I got a good look at one of my pursuers, a tall white male in his late twenties or early thirties. He tried to keep the door open but it closed on him.

Once I reached the lobby floor, I calmed down and tried to walk out without catching anyone's eye. I had to get on another damn line to leave! After a few minutes or so, there were only two people ahead of me now. I kept my eye on the elevator door that brought me up, to make sure they didn't follow me. All of a sudden, the person directly in front of me was having trouble with their card going through the reader. I heard an elevator ding and the doors open. I swung my head around and saw the same tall white guy and company in tow, coming off the elevator. I knew I was in trouble now. The woman in front of me wasn't budging, so I did what I had to do. I shoved her out of the way, shouting, "Excuse me. I am sorry!" I ran for the door with agents and security chasing after me. I ran as fast as I could to get to the AUV and get out. Q was going to have to figure this out for herself, or maybe she did set me up, either way, I have to go. I got in the car, shoved the key in, started the engine, and sped off like a fire was on my ass!

I got a good distance between the Pentagon and myself, keeping a look out for anyone who could be on my tail. But there was no one. I was driving on an empty road the seemed to stretch on for miles. My destination? The Washington National Airport, of course. I pulled the car over for a moment, I hopped out and ran to the side of the road and puked my freaking guts out! I wiped my mouth with my sleeve, when I looked up to find a helicopter coming toward me, and on the horizon, I could see cars with sirens blaring behind me. I got back in the car and tried to make a break for it. But before I got too far, I saw three black cars were ahead of me forming a blockade. What were they thinking? I don't know, but I am out of here! I ran right through their blockade ramming their cars aside as I made my way to my escape. Two minutes later, a car coming straight

<u>CHAPTER FIVE</u>

at me from the right side of my car collided with mine. It brought me to a screeching halt. When I picked my head up from the steering wheel, my head was swimming. I looked in the rear view mirror and saw the cars that pursued me were getting ever closer. The car that rammed into me was smashed and the driver seemed to be unconscious. That's when it happened, all I felt were sharp needle tips sticking me on the left side of the neck. Then came the shock! As electricity passed through my body, I was unable to control or defend myself. It was over and I knew it. They had me.

Thursday, November 9th, 2056; 9:26pm
Hames' home in Washington D.C.

Hames was sitting at his desk in his basement office speaking with several gentlemen smoking cigars and cigarettes. One of the men at the meeting spoke and said, "Ed, listen, this thing with Bridges is getting out of control. We need to eliminate Bridges and anyone helping him, now. What do you have planned?" Hames responded, "I have him in custody right now. I will handle this situation as I see fit. Is that clear to you? To all of you? Let's not forget who we are. Lest we forget, to respect due my office." He continued, "Nothing will interfere with my plans, our plans for reform. We will sign the official documents of our surrender to the Russians, and we, my friends, will reap the reward of our labors!" A voice said, "I hope so." Hames got up from his seat and said, "Now gentlemen, I have pressing business to tend to. Good night. Trini, bring him in."

When I awoke, I found myself sitting in a comfortable brown leather chair with men dressed in dark colored suits and some in street clothes, standing around me. Then I heard a voice and followed it with my eyes to find a man sitting across from me. He was motioning the other men to move aside and they did. He said, "Glass! Can you hear me? Do you understand me boy?" As my head was clearing, I naturally assumed that I was in Washington D.C., but my exact location could not be determined. As I looked around, I noticed there were no windows in this room. Also, I noticed pictures of people and children. Maybe this was his home. The man rose from his chair and approached me. He raised his hand and slapped me across the face. Yeah, he got my attention. I jumped at him and his goons grabbed me, holding me back. They threw me back in my chair and told me to stay there.

The man said, "Hey…Jackson. Sorry, I had to make you wait for me so long. I have to keep up appearance, I am sure you understand. The leader of the free world cannot just up and leave Senate meetings in the middle of the day or not show up for dinner with his family." I understood more as the conversation continued. Hames said, "Do you know who I am? See," he said speaking to Trini, "see what I have been saying about today's youth? They don't even recognize their elected representatives! Some think of me as the puppeteer. Others say I am the man with the power behind the man with the power. Well, I am the closest thing this country has ever had to a king. My name is---" I interrupted him and said, "Yeah I know who you are, Ed Hames. What do you want with me?" Before he answered, one of his goons handed him my envelope filled with my entire mission. "We found this on him, boss." one man said. "Well let's have a look-see, shall we?" Hames said almost cheerfully. He glanced over each page until he came to the Mission Report. "Humph, what might this be? It's a mission report from that fateful day when so many lost their lives fighting for their freedom. Well as we all know, freedom does have its price, does it not? Did you get a chance to read this as you were going through government owned files, breaking and entering, trespassing on federal property, and endangering national security?"

"Yeah, I read it." I said, "I read about a guy named Thomas Reynolds who just happens to have the same name as a U.S. Senator. Turns out, he actually piloted the bomber jet that was assigned to Capt. Richard Bridges. Apparently, he destroyed that Arab Militia base in Jordan and he was instructed to do so, by one Lt. Robert Hames. Any relation... Ed?" "Point in fact, he was my brother." Hames answered me, "Guys go on. We'll be fine. Won't we Mr. Glass?" I simply stared him in the eye. The Plumbers left the room. "I think you have earned a little history lesson, since you have taken it upon yourself to engage in such reckless and dangerous behavior." Hames continued, "I served with Bridges in '31. Then I was elected to the Senate early'32 and I was working on the Desert Wars committee. You see, the Senate was divided into many groups to handle specific areas of the war, in addition to our domestic responsibilities. My peers concocted a plan of attack that I knew would come back to haunt us in the future. They figured we could destroy the bases and blame the Russians. Maybe, just maybe, we could strike a humanitarian cord among our people and allies. I objected to this, but of course, I was overruled. The directive was set anyway, and my brother was given his orders. Don't be fooled, Bridges would have flown that jet if so ordered, but he was still healing from an accident that happened prior to this event. What we didn't know was members of the American media had found a way to embed reporters with Arabic regiments in that area and videotaped the massacre. The live feed was aired all over the world for Christ sake. Someone had to hang."

"So why not let the real pilot fry. Why did you have to blame Bridges?" I interjected. "Do you know who Reynolds is my boy?" Hames asked, "No of course not. He wasn't just any soldier then and he isn't just any Senator now. He is the grandson of former President George W. Bush. If you are not up on your game, then you should know just how powerful the Bush's have become during the war. A war, might I add, that could have been avoided if either one of them had given Russia the aid they needed instead of leaving them to dry after the Soviet Union fell in the late 20th Century. No, Jackson, one does not leave someone like that to hang for anything because the political price was just too high for any of us to suffer." I asked him, "Why did you accuse him of rigging the elections then? Why was he convicted of treason?"

"I told you," he said, "the political price was high. So was the reward. Because I had the least to lose compared to the rest of the committee, I was considered as a liability. Rather than do away with me, I was made an offer. For my compliance, I would be allowed to use their resources to secure my position and rise among the ranks of the Senate. Eventually a deal was worked out to capture the powers of the President and rid us of the middleman. The Congress was always the real power in this country. But, as long as the President had the power to veto, we were at his mercy. Bridges did not want to go along with my offer to make him a very wealthy man. So, I opted to eliminate him instead. If he had just went along with the plan, but he was still vexed about us using him back then to take the fall for Reynolds." He continued, "My brother, my peers, and my superiors saw no reason to let one of our own bear the burden of this action. Who cares anyway? He was just another poor Negro that made good. Who knew he would make it to the Presidency? That was a kick huh? But then what do you care about our needs? You are nothing but a high yellow version of his kind anyway." I just sat there and let him talk some more. "You sit there with your hazel eyes, light colored skin and wavy hair enjoying the benefits of your heritage. Your daddy was white, your mama was black, and there you sit, a product of interbreeding! You know, I didn't even feel that bad when I had to give the order for your father to be killed. I knew him for a time, just as I knew Bridges. Your daddy would still be alive had he tended to you, instead of traveling around the world meddling on Bridges behalf."

With those words, I could no longer restrain myself. I lunged for Hames' throat and punched repeatedly. I felt it inside of me. I wanted to kill him right here, right now. I wanted this done. If I killed him what could happen? Maybe the Senate will never be tamed then. His men will kill me for sure, or I will be in cell next to Bridges. Then Hames spoke to me under labored breath, "Wait! Wait!" And so I paused. He said "If you kill me now, my guys have been instructed to kill you and your pretty little ex-wife, I'll burn her alive!" I raised my fist and said, "You don't know where she is." "Fool! *I am the government.*" he stated, "No one can hide from me!" I stopped and slowly, I got off him and rose to my feet, as did he. "Fine. I won't kill you, now. What are you going to do with me?" As he got on his feet massaging his neck, he said, "You can do me no harm now. I have all of your proof. I have your access codes. I have your means of infiltration and escape. You are no threat to me. You are free to leave but you are never to return, nor to make known to anyone what you have discovered. Know this Glass, if I so much as hear a rumor of this anywhere from anyone, I will destroy all you love and then I will destroy you."

I thought to myself, 'good, take what you have Hames, I have the report on my digi-chip and I know there are others who know his secret'. He instructed me to leave and for the Plumbers to let me go peacefully. They did. I cannot believe what just happened. I felt like I was staring a shark in the eye when I looked at Hames. I felt like any moment now, I will be eaten. I paid a cab to take me from D.C. to the Washington National Airport in Virginia. I have to get in touch with Bridges and get the info to his contact, immediately.

Back inside Hames' home

"Sir," one of Hames' Plumbers said, "Director Harris is here to see you." Hames responded, "What? Why? What does he want now?" "Well sir," the goon continued, "he says it is urgent". "Fine, send him in." Hames orders. Harris walks quickly into the room holding a brown leather briefcase in one hand and in the other a manila file folder. He places the briefcase on a table by the wall under Hames' family portrait. He opens it and reveals a portable info-disc player, similar to the DVD players of the early 21st century. He placed the disc inside the tray and pushed it in. Harris told Hames, "Sir, we have a situation. I was informed that you just let Glass leave the premises." Hames said sounding very smug, "Yes, yes. I disarmed him, and relieved him of our property and therefore his duty. Humph." "No sir," Harris proceeded, "look at what our security cameras show. Here's Glass, printing the files. But when I fast forward, you will see Glass taking pictures of those same reports! Unless someone discovered a digi-chip on his person from that camera, he still has the ability to expose all that we have done to Bridges and everyone regarding that event. The cover up and how it was used against him when Bridges was President." "Son of a bitch!" Hames exclaimed. He ran to the door and called for the Plumbers.

"Listen to me. Find Glass and get his camera and the digital chip! Harris! Get whatever agents closest to the area, out there now. He'll be heading for Washington Nation Airport in Virginia. That is how he travels." Hames orders, "Stan, his ex-wife. Make the call and get it done tonight. Efficiency, gentlemen, it is what the American government is best known for, so get the job done. To hell with Glass and his family." The men scramble to head off Glass before he takes flight. Harris gets on his phone and orders his agents to capture and kill Glass quietly. The Plumbers board a private jet headed to Buffalo, New York in order to locate and terminate Glass' ex-wife, Rebecca Watkins-Glass.

Washington National Airport; 11:21pm

I finally arrived at the airport, eager to leave this place. The problem is I still feel a little groggy, like when you wake up from surgery. I was instructed by airport security to wait while my plane is prepped but I didn't think I should leave my life in anyone's hands ever again. So, I snuck onto the field and made it to the hanger where my plane was kept. I could see the guys working on my baby, from the distance where I stood. Nothing suspicious seemed to be going on of there, but why take a chance. I almost died several times in the last two days. After the maintenance crew left, I went over to the plane to check it out for myself. So far, things looked normal. I went inside to check it out and found a gun I left behind. I tucked it at my waist when suddenly I heard someone whisper my name. "*Jackson! Psst...Jackson over here!*" It was Q! I hadn't seen her since this morning, when she vanished. So naturally, I proceeded with caution. She came to me and asked, "Where have *you* been all day? When I came back you were gone and the place went ape!" Q said. "Yeah, but where were you? I went looking for you when I done. But I couldn't find you anywhere. I figured maybe you left me to the agents and I should get my ass out of there. I ran but suffice it to say, I didn't make it. They caught up with me and took me to Hames. They took my guns, my proof and almost took me out too. Hames figured I was no longer a threat to him, so he let me go."

"Let you go?" she said seeming stunned by my statement. "Since when does Hames just let an 'enemy of the state' go home with only a warning? No Glass, there is more to this than you know." "Yeah, I think you are right Q." I grabbed Q by the arm and slammed her against the plane's hull as I drew my weapon and placed it under her chin. I then said to her, "What I want to know is what Hames is planning now. Something tells me that you know. So tell me." She looked at me and said, "I don't know what you are talking about, but if you don't let go of me I will be forced to neutralize this little situation immediately." "Q, you don't scare me. Answer the question or I will put a hole in your head and dump your body over the Appalachians! You know I mean it!"

Q looked me in the eye and said, "Fine. I was sent to capture and kill you right here, right now." "Why?" I asked. She said, "Hames discovered that you took pictures of the mission reports you stole from the Pentagon. He wants you dead." "So you've come to finish the job for him? When did he get to you?" I asked her. "I was planted within Bridges' organization to expose Knight and counter all of Bridges plans to remove Hames and other members of the Congress from power. You came along when Bridges was most desperate." Q told me. I got closer to her and said, "I should kill you where you stand. You are a spy. Why shouldn't I rid myself of you?" I stepped back and cocked my gun, aimed it right for Q's head then she said, "Because I know what is happening in Buffalo tonight." I stopped. "Buffalo?" I thought to myself. "Could really be willing to hurt Becky? My God, he is capable." I raised my arm up again, aiming for Q and I demanded her to tell me what she knew. Q said, "How about a little deal first? You are a man of your word aren't you?" I nodded and said, "What are the terms?" "She said, "Don't kill me and I will help you." "What kind of deal is that? Don't you think that I know you would betray me at the first opportunity?" I continued, "Damn woman! You must really think I am gullible!" Q said, "I am a woman of my word. I don't make promises to break them. If you spare my life, I will help you save hers. So Jack, what is it going to be?"

I thought about it for a minute and said to her "Agreed. But the first time at the first sign of trouble, I will do what I have to. You know, self-preservation and all that." "Okay," Q said as she began telling me of their plan, "The Plumbers are arriving in Buffalo as we speak Jack. Trini is going to kill your ex and the CIA is coming here for you right now. I was not the only agent tapped for this assignment. You're like the walking dead, only you didn't know it till now." I asked her, "What makes you think I am so easy to kill? What, just because *you* found me? You knew I would come back to my plane." "Listen, let's get in the plane and go, now before they come. I gave my word and I will stick to it." Q said. "Alright, let's get going then." I said hesitantly.

A moment later was all too late. The CIA was all around us, firing their high-powered weapons, aiming for me. I fired back in self-defense and ran for the cabin door. As I fired off rounds, I actually saw some of them dropping their guns and falling to the ground. Q followed behind me with her weapon drawn. I guess she didn't think I saw her. I got in the plane and caught a good angle on Q. Just as I extended my arm to properly aim for her head, a bullet shot through the left window behind me, grazing my shoulder and hitting Q in the face, killing her instantly. I watched as her body fell backward onto the pavement. I could hardly think at that moment. But I had to. I started the engine and flew out of there as fast as I possibly could. Bullets pelted my plane all the way into the air, but thankfully, none hit my gas line, propellers, or the wings. I barely escaped into the night air as storm clouds gave me the best cover I could have had. It must have been what prevented them from following me any further. My thoughts now were focused on Rebecca.

I pulled my cell phone from my duffle bag and called her home number. It rang a few times and the "Visual Voicemail" answered instead of her. I dialed her office number but they told me she already left for the day. That's when I remembered she just bought a cell phone so I dialed the number. It rang two or three times and then she answered! "Becky! Becky!" I said to her in excitement, "Where are you now?" "Hello? J-Jack, is that you? Your signal is coming through a little weak. What's up?" she said to me. "You have to listen to me. Something happened, something bad. I need you to do as I say." I continued, "First: DO NOT GO HOME. Go to your mother's or someone else but make sure it is someone you know already someone you can trust. Don't leave or go with anyone you do not know. There some people coming to--" Becky hung up. I redialed the number and she answered saying, "Listen Jack, I know we have been alright sometimes but you need to realize we are through! I am in the middle of something right now and I cannot keep allowing you to interrupt my life every time you call. I'll talk to you when I can Jack. Bye" And that was the last time I could reach her.

Buffalo-Niagara International Airport, Buffalo, New York; 5:01am

I arrived in Buffalo far too late. As I walked through the airport terminal, I saw on a monitor a news report that froze me in time. The TV's blared throughout the corridors, "The house behind me was set ablaze sometime between 11pm and 1am this morning. Firefighters fought the blaze for nearly two hours. They were able to extinguish the fire and found one body inside: a female, tied to a chair in her kitchen with leather belts and severely burned. The woman has been identified as Rebecca Watkins-Glass she was twenty-seven years old. Police are investigating this as a homicide. When we spoke to her neighbors they had this to say of her, 'Becky was a sweet young lady. She always helped me with my groceries and keeping up my house since my husband passed not too long ago. She was kind, smart, and ambitious. I don't understand why anyone would hurt her. She was doing so much for this community, this city. We have truly lost a special person.' Reporting live this morning, Jane Alley for Channel 4 Morning News."

Oh my God! Becky… no. They could not have taken you from me. I loved you. I am so sorry I dragged you into this. I fell into the chair beside me. Tears fell from my eyes uncontrollably. I got a cab into town and went to her house to see it for myself. The place was completely destroyed. It seemed as though the Earth itself was covered in burnt black wood and soot, destruction was everywhere I turned. A policeman soon approached me. He identified himself saying, "Hi. I am Detective Stephen Brown of Buffalo Homicide. Did you know the deceased?" I responded, "Yeah. I did." I told him, "My name is Jackson Glass. I was her husband." He said, "Was? As of when?" I responded, "A few years ago, we got married during our senior year in college and it didn't work out. I just got here an hour ago, you can check it out with the airport." "I will" he said, "Do you know of anyone who might be responsible for this? Anyone who wanted her dead, someone she had words with and it got out of hand perhaps?" "No Detective. No one here had problems with Becky. I would like to help you sir, but you wouldn't believe me if I tried to explain it all. Just listen to me. There is a situation and I do need your help. The people who did this, may try to hurt her parents. You have to get some cops down there soon to protect them. Will you do that for me sir? Believe me, I will give you all that you need to solve this but I just cannot do it right now."

He said, "I will have a squad car baby-sit their house for a while, but you need to come clean with me. Can I trust you are not lying to me?" I told him, "I give you my word. I will tell you everything no matter how outrageous it may sound, I will tell you." He looked me up and down and said, "Okay, now what is their address?"

Monday, November 13th, 2056; 8am
Holiday Inn, Buffalo, NY

Five days passed and nothing troubling happened so the Detective decided to pull the 'round the clock security from Becky's parents home. I got a room at the Holiday Inn Downtown on Delaware Ave and noted that no one has tried to make contact with me since that fateful day. I cannot stop grieving for my Rebecca. I cannot get her out of my mind. I –I have to do something; I can't just allow Hames to get away with killing Rebecca. She did nothing to anyone. I feel like I am sitting on my hands in this mess! The funeral is in an hour, I was getting dressed when the room phone rang. I picked it up and heard a familiar voice on the other end. "I know what you are going through. I heard about your wife. I am sorry. Do you have the evidence necessary to complete this mission?" said Bridges. "Yes," I answered, "but this mission has taken on a whole new meaning now." "What do you mean son?" Bridges asked. "My goal is still to help you but in addition, I will kill him. I want that son of a bitch dead for what he did to her." Bridges said, "Okay, I understand. I am going to give you my contact person. All you have to do is send the documents to him and he will take care of it from there. You have to be careful Jack. You are still being hunted. And the law cannot protect you from your hunters. Do not get caught by them because the next time, will be the last time. Once you are secured and ready, come see me. I guarantee your safety. Q was a mistake, I am sorry. We found out too late who she was and where her loyalties rested" "Fine, I'll be there. Now if you'll excuse me, I have to watch as my wife is buried."

After the ceremony ended

I knelt down at the foot of the grave; the rain began to pour down on me. It seemed like the rain drowned my tears from my face. I apologized to her one more time and vowed to get Hames for what he did. I know that I cannot mourn her forever but I don't see how I could stop. All I felt now was heat surging through my body. My anger swelled within my brain, my heart was beating like the footsteps of a rhino as it stampedes. I want to bring Hames down in more than one way now. I want his blood. I can feel all that my father taught me coming back to me, racing to the forefront of my mind. The hunting, the shooting practices, and the killing is all coming back to me now. I will bury Hames in the grave he dug for me. I will. Becky I promise.

CHAPTER SIX

Monday, November 13th, 2056; 11:50am
Nixon Federal Prison, miles away from Presque Isle, Maine

"I want to thank you for your efforts in all of this Jackson. You owe nothing to me or even your country, but you have accomplished much to help us both regain our selves." Bridges said to me while put out his cigarette. "I didn't start doing this for you or this country. I did it because I knew my father wouldn't sit back and let power hungry fiends rule his life and I won't either." I continued on, "But now, Hames has gone farther than he had to. My wife, I mean ex-wife, had nothing to do with this. She didn't even know what was happening!" "I am going to ask you something, you don't have to answer if you don't want to though." he said, "Did you think you would've reconciled with her and start over?" I responded, "I had hoped that I might have a chance. But I can no longer entertain such notions. She was innocent in this little war you waged on Hames. And now she is a casualty of it as well."

"Let's not forget all of the other deaths this war has caused. Think how many people have died since our first meeting, Knight, Q, and many others from both sides have met their end fighting 'our cause'." Bridges continued, "When I say *our* cause, I am speaking of Hames and myself. I acknowledge that they knew the risks involved. But that doesn't take away from their worth does it?" "No I don't think it does. But none of them mean to me what Rebecca meant to me. Tell me what I must do next to complete this mission. Tell me how I can bring Hames down and get my hands on him." "A 21st century author wrote, 'We are all mortal, everyone who breathes this air and carries its scent are doomed. We are all meant to die.' Are you prepared? This mission could end up costing you greatly. More than the lives of others, it could take yours as well if you should fail or succeed. Are you ready for this? Because you are not stepping into a hole, but an abyss." Bridges said to me.

"Thomas Wolfe said 'you can never go home again', apparently that is the life I now lead. So Bridges, you tell me what the next step is, I'll make sure I live long enough to see the mission through." I said. "All right, I told you to get the mission report and that I would tell you who to deliver it to. Here it is," Bridges proceeded, "he's a producer at

Canadian-American Network. You will email these documents to John Falk at this address: ose@can.com. In the subject field, you will type 'Initiate Operation Serpent Eagle'. He will know it is from me and will take it from there. In a matter of hours, he will broadcast the reports all over North America, which will then be picked up globally via satellite by other news stations. It won't be enough to shut him down but it will start the wheel in motion. I have other contacts, 'sleeper cells' if you will, throughout North America that Hames has not discovered; they have information that will quickly force an investigation shining an unwanted spotlight on Hames and his cohorts. Go to Saint Leonard, a city outside of Montreal, Quebec. A woman named *Agatha Templeton* is the person you will need to contact. As you collect the information from each cell, you must send it to CAN immediately. Wasting time will allow Hames' men to prevent his ruin. I have a list here, in my head. You will write down these names and their contact information. Keep it close to you if you cannot commit it to memory as I have."

"Why can't you simply contact these people and tell them where to send the info?" I asked him. "Security is of the utmost importance. If the identity of my media contact were to be discovered by Hames, there may not be anyone else to pick up the pieces. Each one these folks are putting there lives on the line by just having this information, the danger increases by you contacting them. Imagine if *I* attempted to contact one of them? Hames' people are looking for you and who ever may be helping you." Bridges said. "Okay, but how can I put the nail in his coffin? Little bits of info won't do enough." I said to Bridges.

"No." He said, "It won't be enough, not by itself. The final element we need to crush him completely is the record of my impeachment. Moses has that. He also has the list of all who helped Hames in that venture, monies used to bribe state officials and accounts from which the funds came and went. That was the last ting we sent to him. You will find him in the mountainous region of Tajikistan, in a city called Murghob, near the Chinese border." Bridges continued, "When you meet with these people, you will say one thing to all of them, in private, you will say '*Operation Serpent Eagle has begun.*' All you have to do is get it to John at CAN and it will be the end of Hames and his regime. The world will discover that I was set up and unseated in order to bring about this 'new' America."

"How did you and your team come into possession of this kind of information anyway? I mean, damn you could have put a stop to him years ago. Couldn't you?" I asked. "No." He said solemnly, "A member of my cabinet betrayed me in order to avoid doing time. She told them what they wanted to hear and once it was over she tried to leave the country." I asked him, "What happened to her?" He said, "Hames' people discovered she had been gathering 'Intel' on Hames and his group. She was executed before she could make it to the airport. Before she met her demise, however, an agent loyal to me gathered the information by breaking into her house and downloading files from her computer. Before I was sent here, we met one last time where I divided the information among them and laid down the rules. I got them out of the country, using various aliases before Hames or his spies could pick on what happened. The people I have selected were military, FBI, a judge, and one used to be my house cleaner. I helped them to get new identities and they were gone. All they wait for now is a sign from me. And *you* are that sign.

"Alright, what kind of info do your aides have on them?" I asked Bridges. "We gathered documents regarding the criminal activities of the Senate and the House, as a whole and as individual congressmen as well. Arms sales to the enemy, selling confidential intelligence to the enemy; that was pretty much how we lost the battle at the Gulf of Oman. Biological, and chemical warfare experiments, murder domestic and abroad committed by our representatives, and a variety of crimes all of which are felonious and most of which are treasonous. They knew I was catching up to what them. Hames made the call to remove me and take over. He and his supporters or cohorts, or what have you, they are beyond mere corruption! Thus, beyond our salvation as well. All they want is power and to get it, they *will* surrender the rest of us to the Communists. Glass," Bridges continues, "I don't know if I am on borrowed time but listen to me. I may not live long enough to see this to completion, but I have to know that you will carry on the mission. Tell me you will complete this even if I am dead. You cannot allow Hames and those like him to continue to run the free world. Tell me." I stood up looked him right in the eye and said, "You have my word. I will not allow my feelings to interfere with completing this task, but you should know, its only revenge that fuels me. I will make him regret what he did to my innocent."

"Good man." Bridges said. "On to lighter conversation then. Something rare and interesting happened two days ago," he continued, "my eldest son, Adam, came to see me. He said that he finally believes in my innocence. I haven't seen him in eight or nine years. He is thirty-three now and he's got kids. I have not met them though. I am a grandfather who has never seen his grandchildren." I attempted to console him and said, "The time will come." He looked at me with a tear in his eye and said, "I would trade an eternity in Heaven for some time with my family again. Love is tricky. You never really know what to do with it while you've got it, then when you lose it you'd do anything to be there again, to have it again. You would hold on to it tighter than before."

"Tell me about it." I said, "I have no chance to regain my love. My parents are dead, and now so is my wife. Look, I am glad for you and your son. I have to get out of here. This place is starting to give me the creeps. There are so many new faces all around now, they've got me feeling like a bug is crawling on me." Bridges said, "Yeah. Some of my guys are gone now, replaced by faces that watch me often; more so than they watch the other prisoners here. Go, get out of Maine but don't waste any time, email him before you get to Presque Isle. Be safe Jack, I hope to see you again soon. Here. Take this book and think of me, think of what you are doing when you read it. There are many useful tips in this book. It was always a favorite of mine. My dad gave this copy to me and I feel compelled to give to you." I looked at the cover and it read, *The Art of War by Sun Tzu.* I thanked him and left the prison before my exit would be noticed.

In the Warden's office at the same time.

Warden Atkins is speaking with the voice on the phone and said, "He has been here. My men told me that Bridges was nowhere to be found. I believe he was in the lower levels of the prison meeting with Glass. What would you have me do sir?" "They have been meeting in your prison, under you 'watchful eye' and you are now telling me this!" the voice said, "Atkins, I do believe the time has finally arrived to eliminate Bridges. Get rid of him in whatever fashion you like just make sure it is quiet and cannot be traced back to me. I hope we are clear on this matter." "Yes sir. Yes, Mr. Hames. I will take care of the problem."

Just outside of Presque Isle; 3:14pm

Using one of Knight's IDs that Hames did not confiscate, I rented a car to take me to the prison and back. I looked in the rear view mirror and saw that no one was behind me for miles. I thought I finally had a chance to relax and turned on the radio to listen to some music. I went a few more miles and saw the city right ahead of me when the music stopped.

Suddenly, a voice came over the broadcast saying, "We interrupt our usual broadcast to announce that it has been confirmed. A little over an hour ago, former President Richard T. Bridges died of a stroke while serving his sentence at a federal penitentiary in Maine. You will remember that Bridges was elected President after fighting in the war as an Air Force pilot, where he was accused of killing nearly three hundred men in an encampment within the Jordanian border. As President, he went on to end the greatest most brutal war humankind has ever seen. During his second term in office, he was impeached and became the first U.S. President in history to be convicted and removed from office for rigging two elections and sentenced to life imprisonment, along with a few surviving members of his cabinet that participated in the fraudulent activity. The cause of death is believed to have been a stroke, though he was recently reported to have been in excellent health. Once again, Richard Tobias Bridges, the last of the historically recognized Presidents of the United States, a soldier turned politician, known globally as the "Peace Keeper", is dead at the age of sixty. He is survived by----."

A stroke? Then it dawned on me. Hames did it. My God. He actually killed Bridges. That son of a bitch! I could not help but to feel the pain of his passing. The man was murdered. I wanted to turn around and see for myself, and then my promise to him came to mind. I had to carry on this mission. I have to expose Hames for the criminal that he is. I just spoke to Bridges not too long ago. I can't believe it.

Aroostook National Airport; 3:43pm

I have to get to my plane and get out of this state quickly. I made it to the airport where I hid the car under the shadow of a dark water tower. I ran to Bridget, I figured, why bother with the airports normal routine tonight. I have to get out here. I got my bag out of the plane and I was looking for my own Driver's License when I heard a ticking sound. I heard two ticks; I grabbed my bag and turned away from the plane. In a moment, my plane exploded inside of the hanger. I was knocked off my feet by the blast and flung into the stack of boxes in front of me. When I opened my eyes again, I saw Bridget on fire; the heat coming from her was tremendous. All of that fuel burning feet away from me. I am actually lucky that I wasn't any closer or I would be done.

I got back on my feet to find a group of men entering the hanger. One man, I assumed he was the leader, spoke with a Spanish accent but not like the Hispanics you might usually hear. It was more like someone from Brazil or maybe Colombia. He was a brown skinned man with a muscular upper body, and his hair was black and slicked back into a pony- tail. He said, "How are you today Mr. Glass? What? Don't you remember me Mr. Glass? I am called 'Trini'. You and I have met before, at the home of Mr. Hames. I must apologize for having to destroy your plane. She was beautiful. You just can't find a model like that anymore, not since the war ended. No?"

"That's right you bastard. I remember you, I saw you as I left Hames' place in DC. You just stood there watching and smiling." I said. "It would seem that our paths were meant to cross. I mean look at how many things I was forced to remove from your life. I felt that after beating on you for a while, then killing your pretty little wife and then your boss, it was time we met face to face. See, I do not like you very much. No. You have caused many problems for my employer. And when he is troubled, it makes my job harder. Mira! Do you hear me? You have made my job, our jobs, harder. So I feel maybe we should have a discussion. Just this once." He quickly walked up to me. While I was still getting my bearings, he lifted me off my feet by my shirt and said, "Now gringo, let's talk." His right arm moved back and his closed fist hit me in the stomach, taking the air out of my lungs. All I could do was cough a bit after getting the wind knocked out of me, but my rebellious nature, I spat in his face. Once he was distracted, I swung my bag at his head and then again into his stomach. He fell to the floor. His men began to approach us, and then he yelled out a command in Spanish ordering them to leave. He rose to his feet and wiped his mouth. He looked at me and said, "You know something? You hit like your wife. Hey, remember that tattoo she has on her back? The little heart with an arrow through it. It had your name in it. My animal instincts to mark what is mine took control of me; so, I marked her whole body before I killed her. She was so tight, so very ripe. What did you do to make her leave you, eh?"

Anger boiled within me. I could feel the heat surging throughout as my heart beat faster. I had to remain cool. This bastard is out to kill me. I have to stay focused; he cannot beat me. I closed my eyes, balled my hands into fists, and inhaled deep. I heard him running toward me. At the last second, I opened my eyes and saw his right hand coming for my face; I blocked it and gave him a right uppercut to the jaw. Trini was lifted off his feet and dropped onto the concrete right in front of me. I stepped on his throat and suffocated him. He struggled to remove my foot but his attempts were futile. Until he used his right hand, to swiftly pull my left foot from under me. I landed on my back and Trini got up quickly. He dove on to me hitting me in the face repeatedly. I pulled my pen from my pocket and with all of the force I could muster; I pushed it into his eye. He let out a scream as he rushed to tend to his injury. I pushed him aside and got on my feet.

I hurried to get to my bag and get my gun. I pulled it out and cocked the hammer; seeing it was ready I placed it in the waist of my pants. I strolled over to Trini as though I were taunting him, gloating over my impending victory. Then, he stood up, still holding his eye, he pulled a machete and started swinging it right to left like he was trying to gut me and then he went for my head. I ducked his last swing, moved in closer and pummeled him with punches as blood flew from his mouth and eyes. I knew what was happening; I felt the urges in me coming to the surface. I was going to kill him for what he's done to Becky and to me. I wrapped my hands around his throat and closed them tighter and tighter. I wanted him dead. He struggled to break free, hitting at my shoulders but I could see the life slipping away from him. Struggling to speak he said, "My only regret is… I didn't get to rape your pretty bitch a third time before… I burned her!" And he spat his blood into my face. I moved back, still holding his throat in my hands and pounded his head into the concrete beneath us. I got up withdrew the gun from my waist, pointed it at his groin and fired, twice. It felt very, very good.

I picked him up by his ponytail, and yanked him up on his feet. With his back to my plane, still burning, I aimed my piece at him and fired several times until the magazine was empty. The force of the shots pushed him right into the flames. I grabbed my bag, pulling out another gun, just in case and headed for the back way out. I heard his men scuttle in, so I ran up the stairs to the next level, where I aimed for the ones who scattered about alone. I plucked them off, one by one at first. Quickly, I changed my location after each hit, until I got four out of the ten of them. Then, I found the remaining six of them grouped together, they began shooting in my direction so I ran and hid behind a post till they stopped firing. I hurried back down the stairs, ran toward them under the cover of darkness. I touched one button on my piece to put it in automatic mode. With one squeeze of the trigger, I fired off two-dozen or more rounds and took them all out of the picture.

I rose from my hiding place and walked toward the hanger exit. I reached the door when one of the Plumbers put a gun to my head and said, "You didn't really think it would be so easy did you? We are trained--" The muffled sound of the gun firing into his stomach, sounded like nothing but a mere firecracker. His lifeless body dropped to the floor and his gun fell beside him. I got out of there as quick as I could. My current situation required me to leave Presque Isle soon.

I got to the rented car that I stashed nearby, and it's a good thing I didn't take it back yet. I cleaned up as much as I could and took off; destination Buffalo, New York;

obstacle the Federal Highway Patrol. By now, Hames must have put the word out to the Feds about me. All I could think about as I drove was Bridges and Hames. I had to come up with a plan, I won't last long on my own like this. I need help to get across the Canadian border. I came upon an empty strip of highway and stopped the car. I figured now is as good a time as any to email the report to Bridges' connection. So I did. It has begun, *Operation Serpent Eagle* has begun. On to Buffalo then. I have to get the hell out of Maine.

CHAPTER SEVEN
THE CONCLUSION

Tuesday, November 14th, 2056; 2:30am
Buffalo, New York

I made it out of Maine with little interruption. New Hampshire and Vermont were worrisome, but not an issue cause they never expected me to get out of Maine in the first place. The security in those states was almost minimal compared to where I started. New York was a little different however. I can see the authorities looking at me curiously. I made it through the state by basically going around any major cities and towns like Syracuse, Ithaca, Rochester, and Albany.

Once in Buffalo, I stopped at the house of an old college buddy, a funny white guy we called "Chester", (short for Manchester). He was born in England and it was all he ever talked about backed then. Well, we didn't go to the same college but we knew each other while we were students here. It has been a while since I visited him or any of the guys. We called ourselves the "Dirty Rotten Scoundrels", from that old Steve Martin movie. We were not into frats so we made our own brotherhood. There was Dean a.k.a. Face, Thomas but he called himself "Samot" from the classic G.I. Joe cartoons that aired during the war. Then there was Cameron or "Cam" for short and Jay but we called him "Bronx", because that's where he's from. I was known as "Jamaica Kincaid". They named me after a character in the short stories of the Nobel-Prize winning author, Derek Walcott. They called me that, cause Jamaica is where my mom was from, and I was always on some adventure around Buffalo and traveling New York state looking for trouble to get into. Yeah, that was me, then. Now I am a former globetrotting reporter, turned spy for a dead President.

I rang the doorbell and Chester came to answer. When the door opened, I saw my friend, in his robe and slippers and his curly brown hair pointing in every direction. His face lit up when he realized it was me, and he bellowed out, "Jamaica! Wha gwon mon?! Come in, come on" I have to admit, I was relieved that he was there for me. I politely asked him if I could use his shower and he answered 'sure'. As I went up the stairs, I stopped and said, "Ches? I need your help man." He said, "What kind of help, Jack?" I responded, "Like the old days. Remember how we made some extra bucks to go to Virginia Beach for Spring Break during our junior year? Like that." All he said was, "Oh. Well, the towels and stuff are in the closet nearest to the bathroom door. I'll see ya in the morning." And I went to take my shower.

I came back down feeling refreshed, but still exhausted. Who wouldn't be after the last two weeks that I've had? Chester went back to sleep and I planted myself on the couch in front of his TV set. I don't know how much longer after that I nodded off but that is what happened.

That day 9am

When I awoke, I found Chester in the basement, doing some research for our little project, I went down there to talk to him. "Hey, Manchester!" I said, "What ya doing?" "Looking for your new name my boy." he continued, "What was your mom's maiden name?" I answered him, "Lincoln. You know what I need right, boss?" Chester looked at me, smirked and said, "You, my friend, need the works. Don't worry, before you leave here today, you will have several new names, passports, social security numbers, birth certificates and various state IDs to match." I said to him, "Hey Ches, listen, I am going to need a little more than that. I am going to need documents from a couple of different countries." Chester looked at me strange and said, "Which ones?" I thought about it for a minute and said, "Canada, Tajikistan, England, Russia and China… just in case." "Dude, are you crazy?" he said, "You plan on going into the heart of the Communist Alliance? Don't go starting another war, ok? We are doing just fine the way we are." He paused and said, "Listen, man… I am sorry to hear about Becky. She was one of kind. I always thought you would have caved in so you two could get back together. Man, you really are a stubborn SOB huh?" He said laughingly, but he knew it was true. "Okay, look," Chester said, "I have the ball rolling on this. So, do you think you can fill me in on what is going on now? Since when do you need all this stuff? You are a reporter now, a legit, respectable job. So, come on. What is the deal?"

I attempted to explain the entire ordeal to him, in the hopes that he wouldn't kick me out of his house. When I was finished, he said, "So you wanna call the guys right?

Get them over here and we can do it together! You shouldn't do all of this alone Jack." I dismissed his suggestion saying, "No one else needs to die because of what I got myself into. The boys are living their lives. I came to you because I know you can do what I need and because I trust you, Chester. I got Becky killed, I don't need anymore of my family dying for this." He immediately jumped off of his bar stool and said, "Understand Jack, Becky was family to me too. I want to help. I just can't believe you actually killed somebody." I said, "Well actually so far it has been a little more than one. Even though one of them deserved it for what he did to my wife, it all still feels strange. I mean, when you kill a man, aren't you supposed to feel something? The first time it all happened so fast, I didn't realize what I had done. But last night, in the hanger, I wanted to do it, I needed to do it. I even enjoyed doing it. I am not a murderer. So, what is wrong with me?"

Chester put his hand on my shoulder and said, "Buddy, you can't beat yourself up over this right now. Just remember, that guy brought it on himself. It's like soldiers, they knew what they were getting into; they knew that price that came with the job. What you need to do is stop thinking about Becky right now, and focus on the task at hand. We have to get you across the border my friend. You know what?!" he said while snapping his chubby fingers, "I have *someone* in Toronto, I can have these sent overnight and she'll keep them for you." I interrupted and said, "Hold on. I can't involve someone I don't even know. What says she is trustworthy?" He responded, "Dude, it's Jasmine. She moved there with the kids last summer." I asked him, "You know I never understood why you two divorced. Has she allowed you to visit the twins?" He said, "Yeah, yeah, she doesn't give me a problem about seeing my boys. I send her some money every other week, and she doesn't complain. I miss them though. Hey why don't you go get some grub, take a nap and I'll get you when I am done here." I said, "Okay. Just let me get like a couple of hours. My head, back and leg hurt like hell." He yelled to me and said, "Hey can you turn on the TV and put it on C.A.N.? Thanks." So I did. Then I went upstairs, I sat on the couch and the next thing I knew, I was out.

Three hours later

I woke up to hear Chester's voice more excited than usual. "Wake up man, come one wake up! You gotta move buddy!" he said. I looked at him with blurry vision and said, "What's up, man? Are you done yet?" "Forget about that right now come on!" he said with urgency in his voice. I got up and followed Chester into the basement where he had the volume on the TV up loud. Chester snatched up the remote and said, "Just look man, look!"

A news reporter said, *"Live from Washington DC, we have this breaking story. Two hours ago, we announced that the late Richard Bridges, who was ousted over a decade ago from the Presidency, may have been framed in the air raid that killed hundreds of civilian militia in Jordan years ago. You may recall that Senate President Hames, then a senior senator and Chairman on the Wars and Foreign Affairs Committee, used this incident to investigate Bridges. It was later revealed that Bridges tampered with his election and re-election, for which he was impeached and sentenced to life imprisonment. Now we hear that there is to be an investigation of Hames' activities in this alleged cover-up by the FBI to unearth the truth about the bombing in Jordan, of which Bridges was held responsible. In light of the new information, Hames and other committee members will be thoroughly investigated to bring the truth to what happened that day. If there was a cover-up serious charges may be brought against all involved."*

Chester muted the television, turned to me, and said, "Dude, did you do that?" I simply nodded my head in agreement. He began jumping around in excitement. "This is so awesome! You are actually becoming apart of history. No, it's more than that. Jack, dude, you're changing history!" I looked at him with an expression of disbelief and said, "Man, you are way off. I am a guy caught up in the mix, history would continue on without me." Chester said, "Yeah, that maybe true but you my man are propelling it further like, like…. a propeller! It pushes a plane forward in motion and that's what you are doing with history." "Okay," I said, "then why can't I get my name in the papers for it?" He chuckled and said, "Cause they would probably kill you for it."

"Nah, Ches, they *are* going to kill me for this." I said, "And that is my problem. I can't let them get me too." I got a beer from the refrigerator and dropped back onto the couch. This is one of the few chances I have gotten to rest since this whole thing began. I was going to take full advantage of it. But my mind would not rest; it couldn't, knowing that Hames is out there like a shark circling closer until he is finally under me. Chester called for me. He did it; he got me my "backstage passes" to begin this thing. Alright, one piece of the puzzle is in, now I need the others. I told Chester my plan, "I am going to need to stay in contact with you. How are you on the email? I asked. He said, "Well I'll check it everyday. But I only have a work email address." "No, no, no. That won't do." I said with disappointment, "Come on, we'll sign you up for one for those free email accounts, something that they won't be expecting if they were looking to trace back to me. I mean as far as we know, they have no clue that you are involved. So let's do it."

We got on to his computer and set up an account with a popular search engine and email provider, SpiderWeb.com. "Okay, write this down," I said to Chester, "the email address is *dirtyrotten@spiderweb.com*. We can use the notes folder to leave each other messages, instead of sending actual emails. The password is '*scoundrels*'. Keep this with you, memorize it, then destroy the paper and don't let anyone find it." "I got you buddy boy." Chester said to reassure me. Although, I can't say that I was reassured. We needed to work out a system for deliveries that I may need.

I decided to write a sort of farewell-for-now letter to Ed Hames. I don't know, it seemed fitting, as though the situation called for the final word to be had by, well, *me*. I know the end of this is near, it is beyond me to prophesy when it will conclude, but I can feel it coming. Drawing nearer to me, to us, swallowing us whole like a snake would a field mouse. My revenge will be exacted and Bridges will be cleared, even though it will be posthumously. I feel as though I were entering into my darkest hour, because in fact, from here on, I will be alone in this mission. Bridges is dead, Knight is dead, my wife is dead, even Q is dead. I have no doubts that Hames is out there filling the newly vacant positions within his Plumbers. I know he will unleash them upon me like dogs chasing after a rabbit.

I find myself thinking of the works of popular writers that were taught at school and those I learned over time. Authors such as William Shakespeare, Robert Browning, Edgar Allen Poe, Emily Dickinson, James Joyce, Maya Angelou, Arekah Dunlap, and many others. All of their works are sitting in my apartment in Pittsburgh, with pictures of my family and friends. Faces I may never see again, a place I may never see again. I find myself reminiscing more than usual, like a condemned man awaiting execution. No! I will not don the mask of one who has surrendered to his fears or to the will of my opponent. I cannot allow myself to feel defeated; I have yet to complete this task before me. I have yet to avenge my love; I must set things right as I may die in the coming year... or not. I vote for *not*.

Later that day at The Buffalo Waterfront Restaurant, 6:19pm

Chester and I went out for dinner, seeing as this is going to be my last night in my own country. Now that I am leaving, I feel it more so than ever, I feel like this is my home. I have left many times before but I always knew I could return, that I would return. But I don't even know when I might return to the States. I ordered a steak with mashed potatoes drowned in gravy with French cut green beans on the side, to drink I chose Heineken, an expensive imported beer from Communist Germany. And for dessert, I ordered a big slice of Strawberry Cheesecake. Chester had a big plate of Lasagna, toasted garlic bread, and a tall glass of red wine. For dessert, he went for the vanilla ice cream covered in fudge topping sprinkled with nuts, beside a piping hot slice of Dutch apple pie. As we dined together, quite possibly for the last time, I enjoyed the view of Lake Erie as the rotating restaurant was set atop the Lakeshore Marriott Hotel, the latest addition to the beautiful Buffalo skyline. I remember seeing pictures of what it looked like at the turn of the century. Thank God, somebody decided to put money into rebuilding this city and controlling crime. Now if they would just complete New York City. I probably won't ever be able to see it when they open the city back to the public.

"Hey man, what are you thinking about?" Chester asks while he makes visible the huge piece of lasagna he is currently chewing. "Well," I started, "I am trying to figure out how long it will take you to complete the digestion process you've begun there in your mouth." And we laughed a little. "Seriously, I never thought for a second that my life could have led me to this decision. I never once conceived the possibility that I could be going through this." I said, while trying to keep my voice down. "Look, the Bills are actually beating Dallas!" I said. Chester looked over his shoulder to see the game that he planned to watch at home. Chester said, "Whoa! I bet $300 on this game, the Bills better win dammit." "Hey Ches, what made you decide to stay here after we graduated?" I asked him. "I don't know." He responded and he continued, "Remember I got my internship during senior year, they made me an offer. But I never thought that I would be here this long. But hey, here I am and it was to your fortune my friend!" I had to agree because had he moved away, I don't know how I would be getting out this trouble alive.

We were enjoying our desserts when the game went to commercial for tonight's news. The reporter said, *"We have the latest development in the murder of former President Richard Bridges. Federal agents are on the hunt for the killer and need your help in capturing Jackson Glass for questioning. Jackson Glass was a freelance journalist interviewing President Bridges at the time of his death. Richard Bridges, was discovered to have been poisoned while serving his sentence at a maximum-security facility in Maine. Glass is also believed to be a member of "Blue Freedom", an American terrorist organization seeking the return of the old Constitution and an end to Communism worldwide. He is believed to be somewhere in Maine but could have possibly escaped and maybe headed for the Western New York region. If you spot this man, call this number or your local authorities. Please do not approach as he considered armed and very dangerous. We have footage from the White House: (U.S. President Todd speaking)* 'Jackson Glass is our number one suspect in the murder of Richard Bridges, we cannot allow terrorists, be they domestic or foreign, to harm U.S. citizens. Glass must be made to answer for his crime. He is public enemy #1. We ask for your assistance in his swift capture before he harms someone else.' *This is channel 8 News, I am Barbara Locke."*

Suddenly my picture appeared on the screen behind the anchor lady and then they superimposed it to take up the entire screen. There I was! Hames came up with a way to find me. I am wanted for killing Bridges! I grabbed Chester's wrist and in a low but very forbidding tone I said, "It is time for us to leave, NOW!"

There was no time to go back to his house for anything. It was clear that now is the time to make my run to Canada or else I was guaranteed to captured here in Buffalo. Chester and I parted ways with what started as a handshake and became a heartfelt embrace between brothers. He gave me his car keys and said he'll take the bus home. His parting words were "Get across that border. Once you make it, do not look back for any reason. Just keep going. All that you need will be waiting for you in Toronto. Just make it there. Okay?!" And as he boarded the bus, he looked and said to me, "Remember – What dreams may come! Good luck, Jack." And again, I was alone in my mission.

As I approached the Peace Bridge, I prepared myself mentally for my upcoming encounter with US Border Patrol. Then, I gave thought to my friend, my only friend left in the world, Chester. He lived up to his end and sent off what I needed and left me with some items I am in need of presently. I also thought about the life I was leaving behind by crossing the bridge into another country, another life, even another realm. I could not contact anyone at home, for fear of placing them in danger. I had to abandon the position I worked so hard to gain as a journalist. But before I go, I can release the name of the one who the cover up in Israel protected. I emailed that last tidbit to Bridges' contact at CAN. I also asked the contact to deliver a letter to Hames. I tried to imagine his face at the thought of me escaping his grasp. I bet he wish he shot me back in DC now.

Washington DC, Jackson's email made it to the press and the note was delivered by messenger to the hands of Edward Hames at his office. The note read:

"Hi Ed. Are you surprised to get this from me? I hope so. I hope you are starting to see, to understand that you are not Bridges, you are not Lincoln, and you are no Kennedy. You have assassinated another President but you will never be President. You are not untouchable. I will see you in time; I hope you think of me at your retirement party. I am going to bury you like I did everyone you have sent after me. You will pay for my wife and Bridges. Goodbye. Happy hunting and by the way – Operation Serpent Eagle

has begun. *"* Hames said in a panic-stricken voice, "Oh my God. He knows. Glass needs to be found now! NOW! NOW!"

Back at the border.

As I approached the Patrolman, I have to admit I was worried that pictures of me might have been circulated among them and I would be snagged as soon as they looked at me. In the years before the Great War, a person could simply drive passed the border patrol and not give it another thought. But since then, they have become increasingly rigid about checking everyone entering and leaving the country. I drove up to the booth where the Border Patrol agent sat and gave him my ID card. "Name." he said in a monotone voice, as he began to scan the holograph picture on the back on my ID. I said, "Lincoln Stewart." He then leaned toward me handing me back my card.

He asked me the routine questions, "State your citizenship." I said, "American". He looked at me as if my face may have been familiar to him. Then he asked me, "What is your purpose for entering Canada today?" I said to him, "I am going to Montreal, to visit my relatives for a few days." All of a sudden, a voice came over his radio sounding more like static than a human's voice. He said, "ATTENTION! ATTENTION! BE ADVISED WANTED POSTING IS BEING CIRCULATED VIA FAX. BE ON THE LOOKOUT FOR JACKSON GLASS, DESCRIPTION IS AS FOLLOWS: HE'S BETWEEN 5'11" & 6 FEET; MEDIUM BUILD, BLACK MALE WITH A LIGHT COMPLEXION, CURLY BROWN HAIR AND GREY EYES. HE MAY BE DRIVING A RENTAL FORD AUV, BLUE WITH SILVER STREAK ON SIDE. POSTING IS BEING FAXED NOW."

Thank God, he didn't ask me to remove my sunglasses; but I have to get going before my picture comes through on that machine! He looked at me again and leaned into the booth. Just then my mind was racing – should I just make a run for it into Canada? No, they'll bring me back to the Feds anyway. Ok he is coming back now; he might have his weapon drawn. With that thought, I reached for my piece and wrapped my finger around the trigger. The Patrolman leaned back toward me and said "Ok, have a good day. Move on." A deep sigh of relief quietly came over me as I tried to play it cool. I started moving along when I saw my face coming out the fax machine right next to the Patrolman. As soon as I cleared the booth's exit, I sped up, heading to the Canadian border where I passed through without a hitch. Now, to find my next contact.

The Saga continues….

In "**The Ninth Ground: Operation Serpent Eagle**".

ABOUT THE AUTHOR

Born Charles G. Smith III in Brooklyn, NY on January 21, 1977, the man who would adopt the attribute Abd' al Halim K. Rashad was raised on Reggae and American Pop music. Born to a Jamaican family, Halim bore witness to the atrocities of life growing up with an abusive father. Then in his teen years, he learned of that other music out there that was making waves across the nation: Rap music. The only artists he really knew about were The Fat Boys, Run DMC *and all the other popular names*. Later, he was introduced to Audio Two's "Milk is Chillin'" by his cousin. That was when his perception of Rap music changed forever. That very summer at the age of eleven, Halim wrote his first rap song.

Halim's influences are The **Almighty Jehovah**, himself, Da M.A.D.ness, Tupac Shakur, Redman, Method Man, Gangstarr, DPGC, EPMD and Rakim. His literary influences include: Samuel Clemens, Earnest Hemingway, William Golding, Spike Lee, Edgar Allen Poe, Robert Browning, William Shakespeare, and V.S. Naipaul. Halim developed his skills as a Scribe to become a feature **hardcore, battle style** artist in NYC's underground Rap scene. He is one of the two founding members of **Da M.A.D.ness**, a rap group formed in 1993 that had a membership roster of artists from NY to VA. Halim is an entrepreneur; he founded his own independent label in 1995 called, "Me Against Dem/ M.A.D. Labels", which he closed back in 1998. But in the year 2000, Halim established his most prominent venture yet "**Urban Legends Muzik**". ULM is an "indie" record label based in New York City that would only sign the most talented and charismatic artists in the tri-state area. When things went sour with his artists in 2002, Halim decided to shut down ULM and move on.

Halim became known widely as the emcee that rips his performances on stage as well as in ciphers. The emcee that has written well over **seven hundred songs** and remains **undefeated** in battles with a record of **49 consecutive wins to 1 loss** (from his first battle ever). Halim strives to enlighten and educate his fellow musicians to ins and outs of this game called life, more specifically the business of music. At the age of 16, Halim was arrested for assault and armed robbery. When in fact, someone attempted to rob Halim and he was forced to defend himself against his assailant. By his 18th birthday, Halim was cleared of all charges and the case was dismissed. Halim then moved to Newport News, VA to marry the mother of his first child. Three years later the marriage ended on bad terms and Halim was granted custody of his daughter. In 1999, Halim moved back to NYC to pick up where he left off. By then, life had taught him a great deal of important lessons. In 1999, Halim youngest daughter was born. His children have been his pride and joy ever since.

Today, Halim is a father, husband, poet, emcee, and educator. He has worked with members of *Wu-Tang Clan*, interned at the legendary *Cold Chillin' Records* at the age of fourteen, and taught the art songwriting to many developing artists. As of late, Halim has been writing poetry and novels also. He has completed a collection of poetry titled, "Blurred Rephlekshunz, Vol. I; The Foul Doctrine" which, in fact, took more than ten years to create. At present, Halim is working on a collection of novels, and a part two of the Blurred Rephlekshunz volumes.

The future, Halim is looking into starting several businesses over the next ten years, including a publishing company, an entertainment law firm, and a citywide after-school program that will offer college credits, scholarships and more to high school students. Halim's main goal is to offer a new medium for the youth to utilize in the ongoing effort to improve their lives. Halim is looking to expand his gifts to guiding the next generation to improving their "choice making" ability. Life is not a music video, but the youth are suffering from this illusion. When they suffer, we also suffer.

Currently, Halim is married (again), father of 3, and student at Buffalo State College. Halim majors in English (B.A. degree) and Criminal Justice (B.S. degree). After college, Halim plans to attend Law school to become an entertainment attorney and remain an entrepreneur.